KEEPERS OF THE KHYBER

THE APEX SERIES

For Boys

KIDNAPPED IN CORNWALL
By Percy Woodcock

KEEPERS OF THE KHYBER
By Arthur Catherall

ON MY RIGHT . . .
By James W. Kenyon

THE IMPOSSIBLE PREFECT
By Hubert Robinson

For Girls

ANN THORNE IN AMERICA
By Rosamond Bertram

THE FAMILY AT SUNSHINE RANCH
By Helen Dickson

THE ADVENT OF ANNE
By Janet Grey

THE HARLANDS GO HUNTING
By Phyllis I. Norris

A QUIET TIME FOR MOLLY
By Norah Pulling

ANN THORNE—REPORTER
By Rosamond Bertram

"Back to the far wall," Clay snarled.
(*See page* 186.)

iv

KEEPERS OF THE KHYBER

by

ARTHUR CATHERALL

Illustrated by R. T. Cooper

THOMAS NELSON AND SONS LTD
LONDON EDINBURGH PARIS MELBOURNE
TORONTO AND NEW YORK

THOMAS NELSON AND SONS LTD
Parkside Works Edinburgh 9
3 Henrietta Street London WC2
312 Flinders Street Melbourne C1
5 Parker's Buildings Burg Street Cape Town

THOMAS NELSON AND SONS (CANADA) LTD
91–93 Wellington Street West Toronto 1

THOMAS NELSON AND SONS
19 East 47th Street New York 17

SOCIÉTÉ FRANÇAISE D'EDITIONS NELSON
25 rue Henri Barbusse Paris Ve

CONTENTS

KEEPERS OF THE KHYBER

CHAPTER ONE

A SWAGGERING Afridi sauntered down the Street of the Storytellers in the old city of Peshawar. He was tall, light brown of face, and had the wide shoulders of one born and bred in the naked hills of the Khyber. There was an arrogant smile on his face as he brushed past a waxen-faced Hindu. A sweating Babu stepped aside to avoid him as he walked across to where a dealer in Turkestan carpets offered his wares.

In that crowded thoroughfare were gathered men from every corner of Asia within three hundred miles of the Safed Koh hills. Wandering about like homeless dogs were the swarthy-skinned Provindahs—wild, beggarly-looking men, whose tribe has carried goods between India and Afghanistan for the past hundred years. Hindus squatted behind piles of green tea, bags of grain, and metalware from far-off Birmingham. On every side dealers waited to sell the wealth of central Asia and India. By a turn of the head a man could see Astrakhan pelts from Khorasan and silks from Bokhara, while the air throbbed with the tap-tap-tap of hammers from the nearby coppersmiths' bazaar, where craftsmen shaped pots and pans from sheets of shiny metal.

To all appearances the big Afridi was one among many other untamed hillmen, but behind his broad forehead was the keen brain of Bill Night of the Secret Service.

For four days Bill Night had prowled this city of a thousand crimes. He had listened to rumours which circulated swiftly from lip to lip, starting no one knew where. Not one man in those crowded bazaar streets but knew that John Staines, Political Agent for the Khyber Pass, was missing.

John Staines was the man who acted as link between the tribesmen and the British soldiers who kept open the Khyber Pass road. He had the delicate task of meeting the warlike Maliks or headmen and listening to any complaint they had. He paid over to them the tribute money exacted from all traders passing through the Khyber to either Afghanistan or to India.

Four days ago his servant had gone in with a morning cup of tea to find the room in disorder and

John Staines missing. The Political Agent had been abducted.

Bill Night stood for a few moments looking down at the carpets which a brown-faced man offered for sale. He sneered as the dealer began to recite the merits of his wares, and extolled their amazing value. Bill Night was not looking at the carpets ; he was watching the man's eyes. The dealer gabbled on, giving the history of the beautiful examples of Turkestan art, and at the same time he winked . . . once, twice, and up to five times.

The carpet was lifted three times, and none of the other men gathered about them knew that a message had passed between the dealer and the Afridi. Bill Night rasped out a snarling, bitter tirade about the price of the carpets, and turned on his heel with a contemptuous laugh.

Dusk was falling. The polyglot crowd was thinning a little. Evil smelling pi-dogs darted about, snatching mouthfuls from the garbage which littered the streets, yelping as they were kicked in their gaunt ribs.

Bill Night walked slowly down the Street of the Storytellers, passed the entrance to the Street of the Houris, counted four more alleyways, and turned down the fifth. Five winks meant he must turn into the fifth alley. Three times the carpet had been lifted; he must enter the third house if he would learn something of the missing John Staines.

No ordinary white man would have dared to enter that gloomy stinking room, where the worst elements of Peshawar gathered for relaxation. Men were drinking *bhang*, a liquor which brought out the worst instincts in the drinkers, so that stabbing affrays were common enough in haunts such as this. A chorus of half-strangled coughs from one corner told Bill that *charas* addicts were smoking the evil essence garnered from the crushed leaves of the hemp plant.

Bill called for a hubble-bubble pipe, and was soon adding a little more smoke and smell to the thick atmosphere. As he sat and puffed, his eyes and ears were busy. Bill Night had been drafted out of the army several years before because of his amazing knowledge of languages and his equally wonderful grasp of native customs and habits. These, with a courage which never allowed him to admit defeat, had already brought to nothing several plots which might have set the frontier aflame. His name was never associated with his deeds in print, but his superiors had been heard to say that Bill Night with his assistant was worth a brigade of troops and a squadron of bombing 'planes in the Khyber Pass area.

Sucking leisurely at his hubble-bubble pipe Bill looked about him. Clay Armstrong, his partner, at that moment pretending to sell Turkestan carpets in the bazaar, had intimated that in this evil-smelling den some information might be obtained. Clay seldom made mistakes. He was a wizard where gleaning news was concerned. No one seemed to know his real Christian name. He had been a drummer boy, and his nickname of " Pipeclay " had gradually been reduced to " Clay."

Here, then, Bill saw Afghan tribesmen from the Ghazni hills, men from Yarkand and the Black Mountain. In the far corner sat a Semite from Merv, with black corkscrew curls peeping from beneath his skullcap. Bill decided this man might be worth watching : he was alone, and neither smoked nor drank ; therefore he might have special business which could be carried on only in such a place.

The most-used tongue in this babel of languages was Pushtu. Bill listened, his senses alert for the first hint that he might be on the track of John Staines. Then a dog yapped shrilly from the dark alley. Bill's teeth clipped hard on the stem of his pipe ; the sound was not the high-pitched bark of a pi-dog, but the shrill eager note of an excited terrier. Bill waited, senses alert. Clay must have left his carpets; his signal told his chief that a suspect was going to enter the den.

A few moments later a tall man entered—apparently one of the foppish youths who come from the plains to Peshawar from time to time to " see life." He sported a rose behind his ear, and Bill's nostrils wrinkled as he sniffed the cloying scent of heavy oil from the man's hair. He noticed that the new-comer was nervous.

The latter stood for a moment surveying the crowded room ; then he saw the Semite in the far corner, and hurried across to him. The two men began an earnest conversation. Bill watched for an opportunity to get nearer. It came after a lapse of five minutes. A Zakka Khel tribesman, who had drunk too much *bhang*, began to quarrel with one who stood by. A knife was drawn, but before it could be used the Zakka Khel was struck from behind, knocked senseless, and hurried through a back door. When the man awoke he would probably be in some stinking cul-de-sac, robbed of his few possessions.

Bill moved nearer the Semite and his friend, but though he strained his ears he heard nothing. Then

14

the youth rose, made a slight obeisance to the Semite, and left by the way he had come. Bill let him go, knowing that Clay would attend to him. The Semite turned to the back door. Bill followed a few seconds later, and hurried after his quarry through the twisting garbage-littered alleys which criss-crossed behind the bazaars.

The Semite went to the caravanserai, where grumbling camels lay cheek by jowl with patient ill-treated donkeys. For three hours Bill dogged the man's footsteps, until he felt fairly certain that he knew just which camels belonged to him ; as the caravan could not leave for the Afghan border before Friday, he was confident that should the need arise he could lay hands on the Semite without much trouble.

When the latter had gone he searched the camel packs, taking care to return every article to its proper place. He discovered nothing, and was weary and somewhat dispirited as he made his way back to the bungalow in Peshawar cantonment, where he and Clay lived when duty permitted.

Clay was waiting for him, dressed now in ordinary clothing. The ex-drummer boy was excited ; he forgot his instructions never, on pain of being kicked in the pants, to call Bill " sir."

"Heard the news, sir ? " he began, as Bill entered the room.

"Heard nothing," grunted Bill. " Heard nothing and seen nothing. You had better luck ? "

" Yes, sir."

" Bill to you."

" Yes, sir . . . Bill," Clay resumed. " First of all, Mr. Staines has returned."

"What ? " Bill was on his feet immediately. " When ? What's happened to him ? Is he all right ? "

" That's the funny part of it, sir—Bill," Clay replied. " He doesn't know a thing. Remembers being attacked while he was in bed. Then he thinks he was drugged . . . because the next thing he remembered was waking up on the Jamrud-Peshawar road this morning. He's a bit shaken, but the doctors say he'll be all right after a night's rest."

" So all our chasings about in the bazaars have been for nothing ? " Bill growled.

" No, Bill," Clay assured him. " There's something fishy going on, which concerns the Khyber Pass railway. I heard a whisper to-day which proves it."

" Sit down, Clay," said Bill, suddenly more cheerful, " and take the weight off your feet. Now what's this fishy smell which makes you think there's trouble brewing in the Pass ? "

Clay sat down.

" That painted fop whom I followed this afternoon —the fellow who came to find the Semite—was stopped almost opposite my carpet stall. Two Afridis insisted on talking to him, and from what I gathered the landslide in the Ali Masjid Gorge which the Malik Din Khels repaired was not an accident. It was caused by a bomb."

" Go on, Clay, this sounds interesting," Bill said, his eyes narrowing. "I know the engineers couldn't understand why there should be a landslide, but they didn't suspect sabotage."

" I presume you followed that Semite bloke," Clay went on. "I followed the Hindu again after he left that drinking place. He met the two Afridis again, and I distinctly heard him say : ' After Saturday ' and they seemed satisfied then. He's a clerk in the baggage department at the railway station."

Bill sat in silence for a minute or two, and his eyes held an excited gleam when he spoke.

" On Saturday there's a hefty consignment of rupees going up the Pass by rail—the wages due to the Malik

Din Khels for their work on the alleged landslide.
Two hundred of 'em worked for three weeks on that
job. Now I wonder if some blighter is thinking of
trying to grab the money."

Clay gasped.

" They wouldn't dare try to rob a military train,"
he said. " Why—they—they couldn't."

Bill shook his head grimly.

" Clay, an Afridi would rob Shaitan himself if he
thought he could get money for rifles and ammunition
by so doing. Besides, somebody may be wanting to
get a smack in at the Malik Din Khels, by robbing
them of their hard-earned wages."

Clay nodded. There is little love lost between the
tribes which occupy the Khyber Pass area. Blood
feuds are carried on night and day between men who
live within a stone's throw of each other, and it would
be a tale for the whole of the Khyber to laugh over if
the Malik Din Khels were robbed of money earned
while working for the hated *Feringhi*.

Next day Bill went to see John Staines, but was
informed that the Political Agent had been ordered
several days' complete rest by his doctor, and was
therefore receiving no visitors at all. Bill therefore
went ahead with his own arrangements. The suspected

railway clerk was to be watched day and night by a white plain-clothes policeman. Clay Armstrong was detailed to follow the Semite until assured that the man had crossed the border into Afghanistan. In addition, the headmen of the Malik Din Khels were to be brought to Peshawar, so that their wages could be handed over in the security of the cantonment. Bill sent a note to Staines, giving these details, and the Political Agent sent a short typewritten letter back agreeing with all that had been done.

Saturday morning saw a somewhat abashed Clay Armstrong back in Peshawar. He had been tricked into losing sight of the Semite, and did not know whether the man had actually crossed into Afghan territory or not. Bill clapped him on the shoulder, and laughed.

"Nothing to worry over, Clay. Everything is going to be all right. Old Malik Sher Khan and his henchmen have been brought to Peshawar, and they're even now counting out the rupees. They'll be handed over, and the tribesmen themselves will travel in the train along with the Political Agent."

Bill was prevented from reaching the station in time to see the money go out on the military train which was taking supplies to the brigade of troops stationed at Landi Kotal at the top of the Khyber Pass.

Clay Armstrong was there before him, and told him that Staines had supervised the loading, sitting in the compartment and looking none too well.

"He rather barked at me when I asked him if he was fit," said Clay, "so I kept my distance. But with Staines and six tribesmen to guard the boxes, the fellow who pinches it will have to be an invisible man, Houdini, Raffles, and Robin Hood as well."

"Yes, I think we've taken sufficient precautions," murmured Bill. "You can bet your boots that while the train is climbing the gradient from Jamrud to Shahgia old Malik Sher Khan and his toughs will be like cats on hot bricks, watching from the carriage windows. Now let's go to the baggage office."

The rupees being safely disposed of, they meant to interrogate the Hindu railway clerk, and discover if they could his connection with the mysterious Semite, who had found it expedient to disappear from the caravan bound for the Afghan border before that spot was reached.

Along with the plain-clothes policeman who had been detailed to watch the clerk they entered the baggage office. It was empty.

" He hasn't left the building, sir," the plain-clothes man asserted. " I've watched his door like a ferret watching a rabbit-hole."

" A ferret doesn't watch a rabbit-hole," chuckled Clay Armstrong. " At least, not the ferrets I knew when I went rabbiting on the banks of the Ribble, near Preston. The ferret went into the hole."

The plain-clothes man grunted, but made no other reply. The room was searched, and a few minutes later the unfortunate clerk was discovered behind a pile of baggage, quite dead. One glance at his contorted body told Bill that the man had been poisoned.

" Somebody knew this fellow was under suspicion," Bill said after a moment, " and decided to close his mouth. Clay, I've got an idea there's something bigger than a mere robbery behind this business. Yet the Border seems quiet enough. I've heard no rumour of another rising, or anything like that for some time."

" There was some talk of a new Mullah," Clay put in. " But that was about all I could gather. Some mysterious Mullah who was going to do the usual stuff, lead the tribesmen into India, and all that rot."

Bill gave instructions for the body to be moved, and asked the police not to let the matter get abroad for a day or so. He waited at the railway station until word came through that the Malik Din Khel tribesmen, along with John Staines, had left the train at the Ali Masjid Gorge station and gone up to Sher Ali Khan's village. When a tribe had done work for the British and been paid, it was customary for them to arrange a little *tamasha* or entertainment for the Political Agent who had arranged things. John Staines would be suitably honoured with coffee, small cakes, and other Afridi delicacies. Later he would be escorted back to the railway, and would board the supply train when it came back from Landi Kotal.

Bill Night was very silent during the walk back to the pleasant little bungalow he shared with Clay Armstrong. Finally he voiced his thoughts.

" I've got a feeling that there's big trouble brewing," he said ruminatively. " Why was John Staines kidnapped, and then set free again ? Why didn't his enemies—and he has a few—take the opportunity of slitting his throat in good old Afridi fashion ? Or, if they didn't want to risk being chased by the troops, why didn't they demand a ransom ? Why was the railway clerk murdered ? "

" Not being Sherlock Holmes," Clay retorted, " I can't tell you. All I've got to say is this : according to the beggars who inhabit these hills, Allah made

Tuesday to follow Monday, and if the job you couldn't do on Monday isn't done on Tuesday, well, Allah arranged things so there'd be a Wednesday following the Tuesday."

" Oh, what a philosopher," Bill snorted. " Meaning, I suppose, that if we wait long enough the answer to the riddle will be made clear."

" Exactly ! " Clay chuckled, then in a more serious tone he added : " I know it's our job to be one jump ahead of law-breakers, but a murdered Hindu clerk isn't in our line. To all intents and purposes the Khyber is as peaceful as a Saturday afternoon at Old Trafford."

Bill stuffed his pipe with tobacco and relaxed in a chair. The hours passed quickly enough as the two men made out reports of their activities during the past four days. Then, an hour after sundown, there was an urgent knock on the door.

" Trouble," said Bill. " I can smell it."

The messenger who stood at the door brought a note from Bill's chief, calling him to a conference immediately.

Bill hurriedly obeyed the command, and twenty minutes later he was facing the man who directed Secret Service operations from Chitral in the north to

Bannu in the south. In silence the great man held out a sheet of paper. It was a leaf torn from a diary. Bill looked at the closely-written lines, and knew he had not been wrong when he anticipated trouble. It was here, trouble with a capital T.

" I am held to ransom," the note began. " The two boxes which we saw packed with rupees this afternoon, and personally receipted by Malik Sher Khan, have, in some miraculous fashion, been exchanged. The boxes were apparently the same, but instead of silver rupees, they each contained a dead sucking-pig when opened in Malik Sher Khan's village. The tribesmen naturally think this is a dastardly attempt to insult them. They are holding me prisoner, and are claiming an extra five thousand rupees, in addition to the ten thousand due to them as wages, as compensation for the insult. If the ransom is not paid in three days I am to die.

JOHN STAINES, Political Agent."

" This note," said Bill's chief grimly, " was handed to the engine driver of the supply train when he stopped at Ali Masjid Gorge on his way back to

Peshawar. I want you and your assistant to start out immediately. You've got to get Staines back to Peshawar. We can't afford to let that whiskered old Afridi, Malik Sher Khan, put a threat like that over. We can't afford to lose Staines. When can you start?"

Bill tapped the ash out of his pipe, and carefully reloaded it. Only when he was once more puffing blue smoke into the air did he seem to realize that his chief had asked him a question.

"Got to think it over," he said. "Can't just walk into the hills and snatch Staines out of Malik Sher Khan's territory. If I were a magician I'd start right away, but I'm not."

The grizzle-haired man behind the desk nodded. He knew Bill, and he realized that no stone would be left unturned once the Secret Service man started on the job. Bill Night had yet to register a failure.

"Do your best, Night," he said, rising. "Let me know if you want anything. But get Staines back here. That understood?"

"Perfectly, sir."

Bill walked back to the bungalow. Clay was turning over a mass of what looked like old rags. He glanced up eagerly.

" A job ? " he asked, and indicated the pile of rags. " Thought I'd get our flea-infested kit out, just in case. Shall we need it ? "

" We shall. We'll be starting to-morrow morning," Bill said, and threw himself into an easy-chair. " We've only got to rescue John Staines . . . he's held to ransom by the Malik Din Khels . . . and we've got to do it in forty-eight hours."

A new day was dawning before the two Secret Service men had completed their arrangements. They had a cold shower, and turned in for a couple of hours' sleep.

When the sun was beginning to make its heat felt, two beggarly-looking hillmen left the bungalow, passed out of the cantonment, and headed for the hills.

CHAPTER TWO

AT half-past three that afternoon two armoured cars entered the grim sun-scorched Ali Masjid Gorge. The heat devils danced above the rocks, and the soldiers behind their armoured shields were mentally cursing the strange orders they had received. They were to drive as near the main village of the Malik Din Khels as possible, only stopping if they were assailed by rifle fire from the surrounding heights.

On the hills, which they had entered by means of goat tracks, were Bill Night and Clay Armstrong. Both men had army rifles of a pattern several years old, but Clay carried a second rifle wrapped carefully in rags.

" A blinking goat would think twice about coming up here," Clay grumbled, as he wriggled along a rock which felt almost red-hot. " Why I ever left dear old rainy Lancashire I don't know."

" Because you wanted to see something of the sun, my cherub," chuckled Bill. " Also you were probably fed up with watching Preston North End lose their matches."

"Sez you," Clay grunted. "Preston didn't win the Cup in 1938 by losing to a team like Chelsea, did they? You've got to get up north for football teams, let me tell you. If I——"

"Here come the armoured cars," Bill muttered, and eased himself among the rocks, the better to watch events.

They saw the two armoured cars emerge from a cloud of dust, halt on the road, and then begin to make their way across the rough ground towards the nearest mud village. There was a menacing quietness abroad. No red-pantalooned women worked on the lean-soiled hillside, and no children chased goats from one scraggy patch of grass to another.

Bill knew the villages were deserted. Once the chief of the Malik Din Khels had decided to hold the Political Officer as hostage he would take his men, women, and children to some eyrie where he could be safe from the might of the British army.

Nearer and nearer to those grey-yellow mud walls crept the grim-looking armoured cars. Suddenly there was a staccato chatter from the first car, a dozen swift puffs of white, telling of machine gun bullets pouring out and pattering against the hard sun-baked mud.

Nothing else happened.

"Looks as if there is nobody watching," Clay suggested.

A moment later, however, two puffs of smoke rose about half a mile away from where Bill and Clay were hidden ; an instant later followed the vicious crack of rifles. The aim of the tribesmen was good ; the watchers heard a *chink-chink* as the bullets smashed harmlessly against the sides of the armoured cars.

The cars were stopped, a machine gun muzzle slewed round, and with a spiteful crackle more bullets swished up towards the tribesmen. For half a minute the bullets sprayed the rocks and scanty herbage ; then the gun fire ceased. At once rifles crackled from various points on the hillside.

"Now, if those heroes down below obey orders they'll get out in a hurry," Bill murmured. And a few moments later he nodded his head in satisfaction as the rear car began to back towards the roadway. Bill then carefully lifted his rifle and fired three shots. "That'll let our Malik Din Khel friends know we are here, Clay. When those cars have gone we can expect visitors."

He fired several more shots, but by this time the armoured cars had regained the road, and they roared off back down the Pass towards the top of the Shahgia Ridge, and so down to Fort Jamrud and Peshawar.

Once more silence descended on the hills, so intense that Bill and Clay heard a dislodged stone rattling down a steep slope.

"Somebody is coming to investigate," muttered Clay. Bill did not reply, but sat upright, an easily seen figure. He knew he was taking a chance, for tribesmen at war have a habit of shooting first and making inquiries later. Bill was banking on the Maliks being less suspicious than usual because his rifle had been directed against the armoured cars.

"You know, er—Bill," Clay said admiringly. "I don't think I'd ever have thought of a ruse like this to discover where the tribesmen were. If those cars hadn't been brought along we might have searched the hills for days without contacting 'em."

"You've got to use your head for other purposes than holding a hat up," Bill chuckled, and then reverted to the Pushtu tongue. "Anyway, no more of this chinwag . . . from now on forget that you're called Clay and that you're a supporter of Preston North End. Savvy ? "

Clay scowled, but made no reply. He and Bill had a permanent quarrel when football was mentioned.

Bill came from the south and was a supporter of Chelsea.

Like two statues the Britishers sat waiting on the hard hot rocks, with rifles across their knees. It was a nerve-racking business. If the Malik Din Khels were suspicious, the story might end at once with a couple of rifle shots. The man of the Khyber Pass seldom misses a shot ; ammunition is too rare and too costly for him to be a bad marksman.

At the end of fifteen minutes a burly tribesman suddenly appeared from behind an outcropping of rock. His hand was on the hilt of his knife, while behind him several rifle muzzles were thrust significantly over a long broken slab of slaty rock.

" Greetings, friend," Bill said easily, while Clay sat impassive, as if the sight of rifle muzzles pointing at his heart were of no consequence at all. "I see the bazaar talk was not foolish this time."

" What talk is this ? " the tall man asked harshly.

Bill laughed easily.

"The talk is that the Malik Din Khels have a difference with the Gorah-log [white men], and that rifles may grow hot on the barrel before long."

Bill's easy confidence impressed the tribesman, but the latter's eyes were still suspicious as he spoke again :

" What want ye on the land of the Malik Din Khels? Men with no evil in their hearts do not walk secretly in these hills. We did not see you climb hither."

Bill chuckled. Clay, had he been in less danger, would have stuck up his thumbs and said : " That shows whether we are hillmen, old top." It was a tribute to their skill to be told that they had arrived thus far without being seen by the keen-eyed watchers of the hills.

" A man who carries such a precious thing as we carry does not stalk abroad like a simple goatherd," Bill retorted. " Take us to Malik Sher Khan ; we have much to say to him."

He held out his rifle, thus making himself a guest of the hillmen, and as such to be guarded until his weapon was handed back. Clay followed suit, but held tightly to the weapon wrapped in rags. The hillmen expected to be entrusted with the latter also, but after some discussion Clay was allowed to retain the mysterious weapon. Leaving six men to watch over the deserted villages near the Pass level, the group of hillmen led the way at a fast pace into the rugged wilderness away from the Khyber Pass.

Bill was tough, accustomed to traversing these

rocky peaks at all seasons of the year. Clay also was inured to this kind of work, but both were thankful when they finally arrived at the entrance of a cave. Some of the brushwood screen having been removed, the Britishers were conducted into a great limestone cavern, which would have housed three times the four hundred souls who made up the Malik Din Khel tribe.

Tiny fires of camel dung glowed hotly in the darkness. The evening meal was in course of preparation ; the tribe was evidently prepared to stay for some considerable time. Malik Sher Khan was no fool ; when he found that the boxes contained not silver, but the pigs so loathsome to a Moslem, he had gathered all available food and made ready to defy the British until he got justice.

Malik Sher Khan was old ; he had seen the Border tribes at war with the British many times, and had joined in the snipings and raidings. He knew well enough that though the white man often lost the first battle, he never lost the last ; yet the fighting blood in his old veins made him ready again to face mechanized units, the bombing 'plane, and the chattering machine gun. When the old warrior's piercing brown eyes stabbed at Bill the latter thought for a second that his disguise had been detected.

" Who art thou, and what seekest thou with me ? "
Sher Khan asked, while men crowded round, listening.

" In my tribe, Malik Sher Khan," Bill retorted,
" a guest who comes unarmed is given coffee and
chupattis before there is talk of business. I come with
talk of business to thee."

Sher Khan's eyes glittered ; then he made a sign.
Coffee was produced—syrupy, strong, and bitter.
There followed talk about everything under the sun
but the reason for Bill's visit, until finally Bill himself introduced the subject of the rag-bound rifle.

" If a man had a rifle which could kill easily at
three miles, what would it be worth to thee, Sher
Khan ? "

The old chief's scornful laugh was echoed from a
score of leathery throats.

" Thou must have broken the law of the Koran,
friend, and drunk away thy wits in *bhang*," sneered
Sher Khan. " Canst thou show us such a rifle ? Or
dost want me to give thee gold mohurs for it to be
brought from the bazaars at Peshawar ? "

The ridicule in his voice brought angry snarls from
the men around.

" I ask nothing of thee yet, chief," Bill said calmly.
" I have the rifle with me, and will prove how easy it is

34

to kill a man, or several men, from a distance of several miles. Can we reach a spot overlooking the fort at Landi Kotal by sundown ? "

An incredulous silence followed. Had this fellow a rifle which could send a bullet far enough, fast enough, and straight enough to kill at a distance of three miles ?

Malik Sher Khan stood up and went to the mouth of the cave. He looked at the sun, then turned and nodded acquiescence.

" There is time, friend," he said, and his voice was less unfriendly. " Thou shalt show us thy wonderful rifle, and prove its accuracy by shooting a soldier when the parade assembles before their flag is hauled down for the night."

" And if I succeed ? " asked Bill cheerfully.

" Then we can talk of other things."

The chief of the Malik Din Khels spoke curtly, but Bill knew that if he proved his point, he and Clay would be accepted as guests and allowed to sleep the night in the cave. Somewhere in that cave, no doubt, lay John Staines, the Political Agent. There had been much preparation before Bill and Clay left Peshawar cantonment. As Bill Night was very fond of saying : " The man who takes a chance with an Afridi is likely to have his insurance policies cashed before long."

The sun was painting the hills of the Safed Koh with a blood-red glory when the tribesmen came out of a last long defile. Below them, like a toy, lay the fort of Landi Kotal, where a siding marked the highest point of the Khyber Pass railway.

Bill Night's eyes were keen, but not as keen as those of the hillmen who were with him. He could just make out the compound where the flag hung limply in the calm which comes at sunset.

Tiny figures were beginning to assemble. It was the colour party come for " flag-down." When the men were assembled a bugle would blow, and down would come the emblem of the might of Britain.

" There, friend," said Malik Sher Khan coldly. This distant view seemed to have renewed his doubts as to Bill's claim. " There are men enough for thy test of this new rifle. Shoot, ere the sun goes and the light fades, and gives thee excuse to miss thine aim."

" Hafed," snapped Bill, turning to Clay, who was standing obediently at his elbow. " Unwrap this precious weapon. These men doubt its worth, and my skill."

In silence Clay took off the wrappings, while the

assembled tribesmen craned their heads to view this marvellous rifle. There were murmurs of disappointment, for the weapon appeared to be a new but ordinary Service model.

Bill loaded the rifle, and slipped on to the barrel a telescopic sight. He squinted down the latter, and breathed a little sigh of relief. The blurred figures down below now took on a definite form. He could see the flagstaff and the men assembled about it.

" Well, why dost thou wait ? " Malik Sher Khan asked impatiently. " The sun will dip below the horizon any moment."

" I wait for that," Bill said coldly. " If I can kill in the ruddy glow of the setting sun, then I can shoot doubly well in the good light of midday."

" Ayieh, he speaks the truth," several men muttered, and there was a general slackening of tension as the men watched the sun's red ball dip lower and lower.

Down on the parade ground the sun dropped out of sight before it vanished to those up on the heights. A bugler stepped forward, instrument to his lips. He began to blow.

Bill watched through his telescopic sights.

" In one moment," he said distinctly, " I am going to kill one, two, maybe four men."

" We shall see," said Malik Sher Khan grimly. " Pull trigger and prove thy words are words of truth. If they are idle boastings, you will not live to see another day."

Bill smiled, and a moment later, as the flag began to be hauled down, he fired. Ejecting the spent cartridge as rapidly as he could he fired again and again, four shots in all. Then he stood back and grinned.

CHAPTER THREE

CRIES of amazement greeted Bill's shooting. The incredible had happened. Four soldiers of the colour party had fallen face downward, one after the other. As the last man fell the others had broken ranks and scurried for safety to the nearest building.

"The man who falls face down is dead," said one of the tribesmen. "Four men dead . . . from such a distance no man has ever shot and killed before."

"See, they come out to carry in the dead," said another. "Shoot again. Let us see more of this wonderful gun."

Bill shook his head.

"No! If four killings will not convince you, I must take the gun elsewhere."

He took the oily rags from the hands of the mute Clay Armstrong, and began to wrap the weapon up again, only to be halted by Malik Sher Khan. The old headman was almost beside himself with excitement.

"Such a gun has never been seen in the Pass before," he croaked. "We will talk of this matter in the cave.

Come, friend, thou must spend the night with us. Forget the harsh words I used."

Bill nodded, and it was something akin to a triumphal procession which scurried back in the fast-fading light to the cave. The tribesmen were eager to know more about this wonderful weapon. Afridi courtesy forbade their asking questions until after the evening meal ; and of this fact Bill was glad, for in spite of an outward composure, he was now very nervous. The " killing " had been a success, but Bill had taken a fearful chance with it. Before he left Peshawar that morning he had arranged for the armoured cars to visit the gorge of Ali Masjid, and for the soldiers at Landi Kotal fort to collapse, one by one, face downward, when the bugler had sounded his call at sundown, and the flag was beginning to be lowered.

The commandant at Landi Kotal had not been too polite over the wires until Bill explained that he would be somewhere up in the hills " shooting." But the commandant was laughing at Bill Night's cleverness when he finally rang off.

Nevertheless, if Bill had failed to get to the appointed place before sundown, the tribesmen might have suggested he did his shooting next morning when the flag was hoisted. That would have been fatal, for no men would have fallen.

"Luck goes hand in hand with the fellow who's willing to stake his life," thought Bill, and by the time he reached the cave he was feeling much better.

The wild, dim scene in the cavern was "romantic" enough to satisfy any adventurer. Hawk-eyed men and veiled women moved about amid a smell of cooking and a clatter of cooking-pots; the air was sharp with acrid smoke from the camel-dung fires.

Bill and Clay sat down, as befitted honoured guests, and waited to be served. They ate a hearty meal, and then Bill would dearly have loved a pipe of his favourite tobacco, but that was out of the question. He sat patiently waiting for the talk to veer round to the rifle.

"Is the army of the Gorah-log being equipped with these rifles?" Malik Sher Khan finally asked, touching Bill's supposedly special weapon with a loving hand.

"Nay," laughed Bill. "The secret is mine, and mine alone. That is the only weapon so made, and the price for others is high. A thousand rupees would not buy such a rifle."

"How many, then?" was the query, while men waited with drawn breath for the answer. If the tribe could lay hands on a few such rifles, a joyful prospect opened before them.

Bill weighed the situation carefully. He had to rescue John Staines, and he wanted to find out something about the new Mullah who was to lead the tribesmen over the borders into India.

" Two thousand rupees would be the price," he said, and smiled grimly to himself as the tribesmen sucked in their breath. Then, in a confidential undertone he added : " The price could be lowered . . . in certain circumstances."

" Aah . . . *how* may the price be lowered ? " Malik Sher Khan tried, but failed, to keep the eagerness out of his voice. Bill allowed a minute to pass before he replied.

" There is much talk in the bazaars of Peshawar," he said quietly, " of a Mullah who will lead the tribes down to the plains of Hind. It is said that this Mullah has behind him many armed men. If this be true a man could grow rich in the cities of the plains, for it is well known that wealth of every kind overflows in the Punjab."

" Ayieh, we have heard this talk too," Malik Sher Khan said, without much enthusiasm in his voice, " but I have seen the Gorah-log fight many times, and each time their victories come more easily. The Malik Din Khels need more assurance before they join a war." Then the old man shrugged his shoulders, " But what has this to do with lowering the price of this wonderful rifle ? "

" I would meet this Mullah," Bill said. " If he speaks with a straight tongue, then will I produce these rifles cheaply . . . and the Malik Din Khels can also buy at the lower price."

After much discussion Sher Khan finally agreed to lead Bill to the Mullah, on condition that the special rifle which Bill had with him should be sold at a cost of one thousand rupees, instead of two. Bill agreed, swearing that Sher Khan was a treader down of the poor, and a robber of the dead. The old man smiled gleefully, for the Afridi is a born haggler.

Sheepskins were produced, and the men began to roll themselves up for the night. The heat of the day had gone, and a nip in the air promised to develop before long into a bone-chilling cold. The tiny fires of camel dung were carefully covered with earth ; in that state they would smoulder through the long dark hours, ready to glow again for cooking when fanned next morning.

At the mouth of the cave several tribesmen kept

watch, all armed with stolen army rifles. At that height there was not a sound from the Pass save the gentle soughing of the wind coming off the Afghan plains.

The sky was cloudless, a black vault decked with glittering jewels. Bill and Clay took the sheepskins which were handed to them, and retired to a side of the cavern where no others slept.

"Don't see any sign of the Political Agent," Clay Armstrong whispered. "Do we carry out the original plan?"

"We can't do anything else," Bill whispered, "if we want to get John Staines out of here alive. Have you got your torch handy?"

Clay fumbled for a moment or so in his cloak, then produced a bundle.

"Okay," he said softly. "You've got the gas, haven't you?"

"Yes." Bill produced several little objects. "It seems a rotten trick . . . but this stuff won't harm any one, and we've got to think of Staines."

"Yes, and the big white chief in Peshawar won't throw out any bouquets if we fail."

"I'm not thinking about bouquets," Bill murmured, suppressing a yawn. "Come on, let's get some sleep. We'll need to be wide awake when the action begins."

Wrapping the sheepskin cloak about him Bill lay down and was soon breathing easily and deeply. He had developed the useful trick of sleeping anywhere, at any time, and waking just when he wanted. It was as if some little alarm clock in his brain went off at the appointed hour and shook the sleep out of his mind. Clay lay down as well. He slept with perfect confidence in his chief. If Bill thought it was safe to sleep, Clay would sleep too.

An hour later, almost to the minute, Bill stirred. He did not yawn or shake himself. Like some wild animal suspicious of danger, he opened his eyes and was immediately aware of his surroundings. Breathing very deeply to conquer a desire to yawn, he quietly sat up ; then he touched Clay lightly on the face, resting his fingers on the sleeping man's nostrils.

Clay awoke, sat up, rubbed his eyes, and grinned in the darkness as he listened to the amazing variety of snores arising from all parts of the cave.

" Like a bloomin' battalion of bassoons, isn't it ? " Clay murmured. Without waiting for a reply he fumbled in his cloak and produced two little gas masks. He handed one to Bill, and put the other across his own nostrils and mouth.

After adjusting his own mask, Bill handed Clay

several small tear-gas bombs. These, when placed on one of the smouldering fires, would soon fill the air with gas.

From the mouth of the cave came a low rumble of voices. The men on guard there were chatting. A rifle butt clanked against a stone, and a man mumbled a curse.

The two Britishers waited patiently. By-and-by the rumble of voices ceased ; the guards were walking about to keep the chill of the night air out of their blood.

Like some great beast Bill crawled quietly across to the fire a few yards deeper into the cavern. Clay went to the fire a couple of yards the other way. A minute and they were back in their sheepskins, snoring in unison, so that if any one awoke before the gas was really thick, suspicion would not rest on the two " sellers of rifles."

The chorus of snores went on unabated. Bill cautiously took off his mask. He immediately screwed up his face as the gas attacked his eyes, causing them to fill with tears.

He waited another minute, breathing deeply through his mask. Then once again he uncovered his mouth, keeping his eyes screwed tightly shut. In a stentorian voice he bellowed an alarm.

" Oh, men, we are bewitched ! "

He knew what would happen. The men nearest him would awake immediately, and make a grab for their rifles. Then they would feel the effects of the gas, and go stumbling towards the mouth of the cave, yelling in anger. In this way the whole tribe would be awakened and struggle outside in a bewildered mob, their eyes smarting, tears blinding them.

Bill was right. Men began to sit up, grabbing their weapons. Curses arose as they threw off their sheepskins and collided with one another.

Choking, clutching their rifles, with tears streaming down their leathery cheeks, they stumbled blindly towards the mouth of the cave. The little camel-dung fires were scattered, and again the embers illuminated the scene with a faint red glow.

Bill and Clay huddled against the wall, preferring to take no chances until the yelling mob had got clear. The tribesmen, with their women and children, took some minutes to thin out as those in the van ran into the cold sweet night air.

Bill touched Clay on the arm, and together they hurried to the rear of the cave. Each torch had been masked to show no more than a pencil of light. Bill took the left-hand wall, Clay the right, and they began their search, the thin beams of whiteness stabbing into every nook and cranny.

Bill found their man. Staines was gasping for air, his eyes swollen and red with the tears produced by the gas. Clay cut the Political Agent's bonds, Bill put a gas mask over his face, and gently they helped him to his feet. He was unable to stand, however; the ropes which had secured his ankles had partly checked the supply of blood. Bill wasted no time, but hoisted John Staines across his broad shoulders. Clay led the way towards the entrance, shining his thin ray of light on the sheepskins and other gear which littered the floor.

Halting about ten yards from the cave mouth, Bill laid Staines down.

"This is the tricky part," he murmured as he crawled carefully to the entrance. "Will they be guarding the entrance, or will they still be worrying about the effects of the gas?"

The night looked anything but dark after the thick gloom of the cavern. The stars in the sky seemed to shine like lamps, and Bill found it possible to see groups of angry tribesmen thirty yards from the cave mouth, wiping their eyes, and gabbling away excitedly.

"It is the work of a *djinn*," Bill heard one man

cry. "Can we shoot a *djinn*? Far better that we move to some other part of the hills, lest worse befall us."

"Thou wert always soft in the marrow," snarled another. "Shall we leave our sheepskins, food, ammunition, and rifles? Nay, far better to guard the cave until daybreak. Who ever heard of a *djinn* which was strong in the sunlight?"

"Ayieh, Abdul speaks well," came a chorus of voices. "Let us watch until dawn."

"If we don't clear out," Bill murmured, as he began to slide back into the darkness, "they'll get over their fright sufficiently to come back to the cave mouth. Then we'll be in the soup."

He moved like a shadow, causing both Clay Armstrong and John Staines to jump nervously when he touched them. Closing his eyes tightly, and lifting his mask, Bill put his mouth close to Clay's ear and breathed a warning.

"Lead the way, I'll carry Staines. Don't even breathe loudly, or they'll blow us to smithereens. They're beginning to get their courage back."

Clay picked up Bill's rifle, the wonderful weapon which the Malik Din Khels were anxious to buy. In his right hand he had a couple of tiny " plum bombs," which would explode like a miniature hand grenade, doing little damage, but frightening an attacker.

They reached the mouth of the cave. Clay's leather shoes—typical Pass shoes, with spikes in the soles and heels at least half an inch long—made no noise, for the young Britisher was testing each footstep. The hillmen were still arguing, and Malik Sher Khan was cursing more loudly than any.

Bill whipped off his mask, and breathed deeply of the crisp cold air. He touched Clay on the shoulder.

" Up the side of the hill," he commanded, " and watch for loose stones."

Clay grunted in his mask ; he had a clear-cut mental picture of the hillside, which he had studied carefully before darkness fell.

Fearing that at any moment they might be discovered, the two Secret Service men climbed. Bill was breathing rather heavily, for though he was a big man, it was no light task he had undertaken. Staines was heavy, and one stone dislodged might bring a withering blast of lead from the tribesmen below. Even the hawk-eyed Malik Din Khels might miss in the starlight, but a random bullet kills just as surely as one aimed by a marksman.

At length, however, the Britishers reached the crest

of that particular hill. Immediately they felt the bitter wind blowing up the Pass from beyond Dakka Fort in Afghanistan.

Bill laid his burden down carefully, shivering at the chill blast on his sweating face. He pulled down his turban to protect his neck and ears, wrapped his cloak more tightly about him, and breathed a sigh of relief. He was about to make a jocular remark to Staines about choosing a better spot next time he was kidnapped, when the man on the ground rattled off a couple of questions in Pushtu. Bill stiffened, the joke remaining unspoken.

" I thought I was to be rescued to-morrow night," the man snapped. " Has something gone wrong ? Has Staines escaped ? "

Bill felt as if some one had poured a jug of cold water down his neck. " Has Staines escaped ? " Who on earth was *this*, then ? He and Clay had risked their lives and rescued the wrong man.

" Well, fool, hast thou lost thy tongue ? " The rasping voice brought Bill back to earth with a start. " Who sent thee and thy companion to rescue me ? If a mistake has been made thou shalt pay for it with thy life."

Bill did some quick thinking.

" Lord, thy servant knows little," he said, his voice humble and supplicating. " One came to me in Peshawar with instructions to rescue thee from the hands of the Malik Din Khels, and to do it this night."

" What else did he tell thee ? "

" Naught, lord," Bill said, and was glad he could find so easy a reply. " Save that we were to obey thy commands when thou wert free."

The man on the ground cursed softly, then groaned as he tried to rise. He ordered Bill and Clay to massage his arms and legs ; and by the time that the first rays of the sun glowed pink on the snow-capped top of Gasherbrum in the Karakoram Mountains, the rescued man was able to rise and walk about.

Bill, maintaining his servant's pose, could hardly conceal his amazement. One important detail apart, this man was the image of John Staines. He had the same curly brown hair, the same stiff brush of a moustache, the same military bearing, the same broad shoulders. But his eyes were dark and fiery ; John Staines had grey eyes.

This man had been kidnapped by the Malik Din Khels ; he must have posed as John Staines at Peshawar when the vanished money was counted out to old Malik Sher Khan. John Staines had been " missing " before the authorities were aware of the fact. He had been removed in order that this man could impersonate him.

This seemed to be no ordinary Border trouble. Somebody was planning carefully, and using men with brains to help him. This Mullah must be found.

Almost as if he read Bill's thoughts, John Staines' double ceased his perambulations.

"Follow me," he snapped. "I am fit enough to walk. There must be something wrong. The Mullah will have the answer to it all."

He strode off down the hill, heading almost due north, in the direction of Kabul river and the dangerous Mohmand territory. Bill looked at Clay and winked. Clay smiled, then pulled a wry face as he patted his stomach ; he was ready to face any danger or difficulty, but he did like large and regular meals. The keen night air had given both men an appetite, and there would be no food until they reached the hiding-place of the Mullah.

"When we get there," thought Bill, a whimsical smile playing over his brown face for a moment, "we may get more than a stomachful. The Mullah will smell a horde of rats when he hears what we've done."

Five hours later, in baking sunshine, their guide

turned off a goat track and began to climb a rough hillside. Bill, looking up, thought he saw a white-turbaned head appear for a moment. For the fraction of a second he saw sunlight glint on a rifle barrel. He turned and muttered to Clay, who was a yard below him.

" Zero hour soon, Clay. We're arriving."

A minute later they were standing outside the entrance to a cave, where Clay was relieved of his rifle and little automatic pistol. The plum bombs, which he carried under his armpits, were not discovered.

The man who had guided them to this wild spot went into the cave, leaving Bill and Clay guarded by half a dozen shaggy-chinned Mohmand tribesmen, all armed to the teeth, and grinning in anything but friendly fashion at the Secret Service men.

Ten drawn-out minutes went by. Then a Mohmand came out of the cave and waved a hand. The six tribesmen closed in on Bill and Clay, and ushered them into the darkness.

They were going to meet the Mullah.

CHAPTER FOUR

BILL Night screwed up his eyes as he walked through the cave, so that when he did enter the inner sanctum of the Mullah, which would no doubt be lighted, he would not be temporarily blinded after the pitch darkness. After a couple of minutes' stumbling over the uneven cave floor he was halted.

He opened his eyes to find himself in a cavern brilliantly lighted by modern petrol lamps, complete with mantles ; the glare was almost blinding in its intensity. The walls were hung with expensive Bokhara rugs. The table, behind which sat the Mullah, had the polish one might expect in the office of some business magnate. There was a powerful wireless set in a corner, and the whole of one wall was covered with large-scale maps of the North-west Provinces.

The Mullah wore the green turban of one who has made the pilgrimage to Mecca. He had piercing eyes and a neatly trimmed beard ; but the set of his face was not Asiatic, and Bill Night decided there and then that the Mullah was a European.

" These are the two men, master," said one of the

Mohmand guards. He bowed low as he spoke, then retreated to the curtained entrance.

Behind the Mullah stood the man whom Bill and Clay had rescued the previous night from the cave of the Malik Din Khels. Bill could not help marvelling anew at the perfection of his make-up. It was very hard to believe he was not actually John Staines.

The Mullah remained silently watching the two Britishers for a couple of minutes ; when he spoke his lips were twisted in a cynical grin.

" Two Afridis with the blue eyes of the British, eh ? " he snarled, " What tribe gave you birth, scum ? "

" Across the Border," came the swift answer from Bill, " a man dies young who insults a Pathan like that. Is a man less of a man because his eyes are blue, and because the accursed Gorah-log also have blue eyes ? We came to offer our services. We have already saved this man who stands behind thee, but a Mullah calls me to no Holy War if he treats me as dirt ! "

Bill knew he was safe in pretending great indignation, for across the Border the Pathans are well sprinkled with blue-eyed men—descendants, no doubt, of the soldiers of Alexander the Great, who stormed their way through the Khyber Pass three centuries before Julius Cæsar invaded Britain.

"Thou art a man of spirit," said the Mullah with more civility. "I need men like thee. Thy companion says little. What is he?"

"He is my cousin, lord," said Bill more deferentially. "A brave, strong fighting man; but his tongue wags seldom. He is a man to whom a secret can be given."

The Mullah nodded, turned and whispered for a few minutes with the man who was dressed as John Staines, and presently resumed his questions. He asked how Bill and Clay had come to undertake the rescue in the cave of the Malik Din Khels. Bill spun a long yarn of the various people he had met in the bazaars of Peshawar. He included the mysterious Semite, mention of whom brought an understanding nod from the Mullah. When he had finished, however, Bill had not committed himself. The description he gave of the man who was supposed to have sent him to the cave of the Malik Din Khels might have fitted any one of ten thousand Afridis.

The Mullah, apparently never thinking that Bill and Clay would understand the English tongue, turned to the man disguised as John Staines.

"Orlof, these fellows have me puzzled," he said irritably. "What do you make of them?"

"I think the best thing we can do is get in touch

with our men at Peshawar. Something may have developed at that end which made it necessary for me to be released," Orlof replied, and then added significantly : " If they haven't been sent by any of our Peshawar men, they're spies."

The Mullah's face twisted for a moment into such a mask of fiendish rage that Bill felt his heart miss a beat, while Clay was sure his face went ghost-white.

" If they are spies," the Mullah said, " the Khyber shall ring with the tale of what happened to them."

He touched a little silver bell on the table. The Mohmand guard appeared.

" Feed these two," came the curt command, " and see they do not stray."

The Mohmand bowed low, stepped to one side, and allowed Bill and Clay to precede him out of the inner cave.

By the light of an ordinary lantern they were given food, greasy chupattis, a piece of rather rank goat's flesh, a bowl of curdled milk. As if unaccustomed to anything better, the two Britishers wolfed down the meal ; they were both very hungry.

A few minutes later Bill pricked up his ears. From the inner cave came the intermittent buzzing of a wireless set. He listened carefully, but though he could make out the individual letters the message, obviously in code, was double Dutch to him.

"There's going to be a terrific row shortly, Clay," he murmured, "when word comes back from Peshawar that we were not sent by the Mullah's under-cover men. How're you feeling ?"

"Fine, thanks," Clay whispered, trying to get a fragment of tough goat meat from between his teeth. "What's our next move . . . if any ?"

"We'll have to leave that in the lap of the gods," Bill returned. "Have you got your plum bombs handy ? I've two . . . and if the worst comes to the worst the Mullah and his pal Orlof have to die. Understand ?"

"Couldn't be clearer," Clay grunted. "Do we shake hands now . . . and agree to be pals in heaven ?"

"May not be as bad as all that," Bill said, grinning. "Never say die until you are dead . . . and then argue until you are in a coffin."

They relapsed into silence. The minutes passed slowly enough. The Mohmand guards occasionally came to take a peep at their prisoners. Apart from the shuffle of their thick leather slippers, and an occasional crackle of wireless from the inner cave, the only sound to be heard was the monotonous drip-drip-drip of water from the roof.

In the inner cavern the Mullah was listening while Orlof decoded a wireless message from the Mullah's agent in Peshawar.

"Know nothing of two men sent to rescue Orlof from the Malik Din Khels. This may be the work of Shushan the Semite, who was in Peshawar for a very short time yesterday morning. I did not see him, being concerned with the gathering of the uniforms you want. These will be delivered to-morrow."

The Mullah grunted his approval, then nodded his head for Orlof to continue.

"Our agent with the Malik Din Khels has reported the rescue of Orlof, and said that the two men who performed this rescue have an amazing rifle. With it one of them shot four British soldiers from the mountain top, a distance of approximately three miles. The soldiers were parading for flag-down at Landi Kotal."

The impassive face of the Mullah creased into a smile.

"Shot four British soldiers, eh?" he chuckled. "Well, that disposes of our suspicions, I think, doesn't it?"

"It may have been a trick," Orlof said tartly. "We can't be too careful."

"You can't shoot four soldiers from three miles away by a trick," the Mullah snapped. "You are getting too suspicious, Orlof. Remember we need all the good men we can lay hands on. These two made a smart job of your rescue, didn't they . . . even if it was ill-timed."

Orlof shrugged his shoulders and made no reply.

"We'll have a look at this rifle," the Mullah said. "If we can promise such weapons to the Border tribes they'll flock to our aid. Bring the men in."

Bill and Clay were brought once more into the inner cavern, and Bill's heart leapt with joy when the matter of the shooting of the soldiers at Landi Kotal was mentioned. He knew then that for the time being he and Clay were safe.

"I can get these rifles, lord, in abundance," he said, "if there is money. The cost is high . . . but when a man can kill from such a distance, even two thousand rupees is not too much to pay."

"You are a wise man," the Mullah said. "Show us this weapon."

Bill shook his head sadly.

"Alas, lord, it was left in the cave of the Malik

Din Khels," he said sorrowfully. "I was about to mention payment for it . . . when the moment was ripe. I am a poor man."

"You shall be well paid," the Mullah said. "In the meantime I shall give you new rifles, and you shall fight for me and the Cause. Soon there will be loot in abundance, and much killing. The plains of Hind, with their rich cities, will lie before us, and the hated British shall be driven from the land."

"Paradise will be but a poor reward for him who can give us Hind," said Bill humbly, and bowed. The Mullah smiled, and Bill noted that this man had in his make-up a streak of vanity—a dangerous thing for any one who hoped to lead the hillmen.

For the rest of the day the two Britishers were allowed to sit about with the Mohmand guards. Over the evening meal they talked of looting and killing they had done, and the Mohmands nodded their heads in approval. Bill knew that Clay and he were now accepted as men who could be relied upon.

When the sun dipped behind the Safed Koh hills the tribesmen made no move to retire to sleep. Instead they sat round their little fires, and after a couple of hours the reason became obvious.

The quietness of the night was disturbed by the

low humming of an aeroplane. The machine came nearer, and Orlof climbed to an adjacent knoll, and fired a Verey light pistol. The blue flare exploded, then began to come down slowly, throwing a brilliant white-blue light over the scene.

The 'plane came lower, and to Bill's surprise several parachutes were dropped from it. These parachutes fell fairly quickly ; it was clear that they were heavily weighted. A tiny flare attached to each parachute marked its descent, and Orlof called out that they were to be brought in immediately.

" What the dickens is this lot ? " asked Bill. " Guns or just ammunition ? "

" If I were a thought-reader I'd be able to tell you," Clay grunted, as he scrambled down the hill behind a motley throng of Mohmands. " If *we* could get a wireless message through to Peshawar we'd have the Air Force here to-morrow and blow this little bunch to smithereens."

" If we did that," Bill snorted, " it would only warn this precious Mullah that we were on to his game. We're doing very nicely, take it from me."

A few minutes later they were helping to carry up the hill one of the mysterious bundles dropped from the 'plane. The bundles were fairly bulky, but certainly not heavy enough to contain either arms or ammunition.

The 'plane made a second appearance before dawn, and once more the mysterious bundles were dropped and collected by the tribesmen. Each bundle was taken into the cave and kept there under a vigilant guard.

"Wish they'd choose us two as guards," Clay ventured. "Then we could see what this stuff was. Felt like cloth to me. Though there were some hard knobby patches in the last bundle I carried."

"Patience," murmured Bill, "is a virtue seldom found in women, and in men from Preston."

"Let me tell you men from around the River Ribble are as patient——"

"As Job," Bill chuckled, "as strong as Samson, as wise as Solomon——"

"And they make the finest footballers in the world," Clay went on, "and I'm not arguing. I'm *telling* you."

They settled down among the tribesmen, and slept for a couple of hours. Over a small dung fire they cooked breakfast, the food being provided by the Mohmands ; then the whole force was assembled in a small valley near by. The bundles which had come by 'plane during the night were carried from the cave and opened under Orlof's direction.

Neat parcels of British army uniforms were taken out and laid on the wiry grass. There were ammunition boots, belts, everything to equip a small force of men in the uniform of the Sikhs.

There were Sikhs at Fort Jamrud, Fort Ali Masjid, and Landi Kotal.

Forty men were selected to put on uniform. The two Britishers were not among the chosen ; through the broiling heat of the afternoon they sat watching while the Mohmands were shown how to adjust and wear their kit, and later how to ride trim ponies which were brought with much labour from a hidden defile not far away.

Behind impassive faces Bill and Clay were seriously worried. When these Mohmands entered the Khyber Pass in Sikh uniform, no doubt they would be taken for Government troops. Whatever blow they meant to strike could be dealt from close quarters before suspicion was aroused.

That night the aeroplane came again, making two trips and bringing more bundles of uniforms and equipment. Bill and Clay were issued with Sikh uniforms next day, and joined the others in riding practice. Both Britishers rode well, and found it hard to appear clumsy in the saddle.

By the following night everything was ready. Orlof was satisfied with his troop of bogus Sikhs, and when the sun had set and the evening meal had been eaten, he gathered them together to give his instructions.

" To-morrow," he said, " the Khyber Pass will be opened by the British for the passage through of the caravan from Afghanistan. That caravan is immensely rich in all manner of goods. Few travel the Khyber who carry no wealth. The Mullah, may his shadow increase, has made arrangements for us "—Orlof allowed himself a satisfied grin—" has made arrangements for us to escort that caravan from the Afghan border, through Landi Kotal, to where we want it to go—which will *not* be the Peshawar caravanserai."

The assembled tribesmen chuckled their approval ; such a trick appealed to their sense of humour. What a tale it would make in the villages when a man grew too old for border raiding ! The British were to be fooled. The lion's tail was to be tweaked, with much profit to those who did the tweaking.

" At dawn," Orlof continued, " we shall ride to a point between Ali Masjid and Landi Kotal. By the time we reach the Pass one of the Mullah's trusted men will have tapped the telephone wires and instructed the commandant at Landi Kotal that a detachment of

Sikhs is coming to escort the caravan, instead of the usual Khassadars."

The Khassadars are a local force organized by the British to protect the caravans. The Khassadar headmen are paid a certain sum, and from this money they pay their men and provide arms and ammunition. The British protect the Khyber on the principle of " set a thief to catch a thief " ; the Khassadars know all the tricks of the Afridi, and raids in the Khyber on caravan day are rarely successful.

" What will happen to the Khassadars ? " asked one of the Mohmand headmen. " If we have to disperse them, word is bound to reach the Ali Masjid fort. Then the whole scheme will be spoiled."

Orlof laughed.

" I shall ride with you as Staines Sahib," he promised. " I shall send the Khassadars back. They will obey the Political Agent."

Again the Mohmands smiled their approval. This was the kind of thing tribesmen dreamed of, but seldom had the means to put into practice. Ayieh ! but the Mullah was great, with wisdom and audacity to outwit even the crafty British !

Bill joined in the chorus of praise, not without ironical enthusiasm. This scheme for raiding the

Khyber caravan had all the essentials necessary for success.

When the men finally dispersed to seek their sheepskins for the night, Clay Armstrong asked his inevitable question.

" What are we going to do, sir ? " he asked. " If this raid is a success it'll be a terrible blow to British prestige. The rest of the tribes 'll laugh themselves into pink fits over it ; they 'll flock to the Mullah's banner like kids going to a free ice-cream stall."

" You're *telling* me again," Bill muttered grimly, " but we can't do a thing at the moment. If there's half a chance of getting out of here, we'll take it. But I doubt if they'll leave the door open for any one. The Mullah will keep his dormitory well guarded, believe me. He doesn't trust this lot any further than he can see 'em. Not yet, at any rate."

Bill's prophecy was true. The entrance to the cave was well guarded all through the night, and when the first pale grey of dawn was showing in the east, and the tribesmen were roused, the two Secret Service men were still with the Mullah's force.

A hurried meal was followed by immediate preparations for the *coup*. The Mohmands donned their Sikh uniforms, and were inspected by Orlof. The latter was critical to a degree, and when he had finally finished his inspection a bona-fide Sikh might have felt justly proud of the detachment.

The ponies were brought out of another cave where they had been stabled for the night. Every pony saddle had its lance-bucket and carbine. The gaily pennoned lances were exact replicas of those issued to the Sikhs. No detail had been forgotten.

Orlof was once again the image of John Staines—spruce, genial, with the military bearing of one who has spent many years in the army.

" The Mullah knows how to choose his lieutenants," thought Bill. " If we scotch the beggar before he does any real damage I reckon we'll have earned six months leave with double pay."

" And we'll get it," Clay said, grinning, for Bill had spoken his last words aloud. " If you don't mind my warning you, sir, you shouldn't speak your thoughts like that. Somebody may hear and repeat 'em to the wrong person."

" I must be losing my grip," Bill grunted, and backed his pony into line as Orlof gave a command. A few moments later the double row of disguised Mohmands wheeled their ponies and started for the Khyber. If this raid succeeded it would certainly go down in history as one of the smartest pieces of robbery ever attempted, and would most certainly encourage other tribesmen in the Pass area to try for some loot themselves.

By about nine o'clock the disguised Mohmands entered the Khyber about three miles north of the Ali Masjid Fort, at a spot where the gorge began to widen a little.

Orlof ordered the bulk of his men to dismount, and rode south with a small escort party to meet the Khassadars. A watching Mohmand had reported the latter as advancing through the gorge a little more than two miles away.

Bill and Clay, at the rear of the detachment, were not chosen as part of the escort. This disappointed them ; for one flaw in the Mullah's plan, so far as Bill could see, was that if word could be got to the Khassadars that Orlof was not John Staines, Orlof might be captured there and then, and the whole scheme nipped in the bud.

"That's one chance gone west," Bill thought. "I've got to think of something else. It can never occur to the Khassadars to doubt the orders of the chap who arranges their pay."

Forty minutes later Orlof came galloping back

with his escort. Now he was grinning, and so pleased that he had to impart his good news to the tribesmen.

" The Khassadars have gone back," he said. " They were surprised to see me : Bazaar rumours at Peshawar report me as still a prisoner of the Malik Din Khels. Later to-day a second sum of money, the ransom for Staines Sahib, is to be sent this way. We'll have that money too."

A murmur of approval went along the ranks. The Mohmands were in high good humour as they re-mounted and moved up the stiff gradient which finally ended at Landi Kotal. There, at the highest point of the Khyber Pass road, a brigade of troops was stationed all the year through.

Landi Kotal was also important because of its caravanserai, a walled-in enclosure where travellers could rest themselves and their beasts in comparative security during the night. As Bill rode up behind the immaculate " Sikhs," his eyes smarted at the glare of mud walls white in the sunshine.

The military buildings appeared to be deserted, save for the sentries at the gates. The great heat of the day was approaching ; officers and men would be seeking what comfort they could in darkened rooms.

"If they'd just be a little inquisitive for once," Bill thought, "they might scotch one of the greatest raids ever planned in the Khyber."

The sentries at the gates presented arms. An order came down the line, and lances dipped in return. Two minutes later Landi Kotal was behind, and before them lay Landi Khana and the frontier, where the caravan from Afghanistan, Persia, and Russian Asia would be waiting impatiently to enter India.

The road fell sharply away; around a bend came in sight the tents and stone huts of Landi Khana. Beyond, as far as the eye could see, the sun-baked plain of Afghanistan shimmered in the terrific heat.

Behind the barbed wire entanglements—behind the great signpost which reads : " It is absolutely forbidden to cross this border into Afghan territory "—was the caravan, a hotch-potch of colouring, a great untidy snake which stretched down the road to vanish round a bend.

Orlof rode to the frontier, saluted the weary-looking British soldier who was on duty in the sentry box a few yards from the Afghan border. He spoke to the Afghan soldiers behind the barbed wire entanglements. The barrier was removed, and the caravan began to stream across into British India.

The disguised Mohmand tribesmen pulled their ponies to either side of the road, while six prepared to lead the caravan through the Pass. The bogus Sikhs were in high spirits, for every man who crossed that fateful border, bringing treasures of some kind or another for the bazaars of Peshawar, was bringing loot for the Mullah and his men.

CHAPTER FIVE

FIRST across the line were the Provindahs, a type of Afghan gipsy who have done the carrying for traders from Herat, Mazir-I-Sharif, and the places touching Persia and the Central Asian provinces of Russia for many long years. They are a genial, wily, swashbuckling type—wild-looking, often in rags, carrying their heavy leather slippers in order to save them for walking about the bazaars of Peshawar. Although their appearance suggests poverty, they often carry great wealth in the form of pigeon's blood rubies found in the hills of Burma, sold to traders in Afghanistan, and then sent to Peshawar for resale. They take pearls from the Persian Gulf and aquamarines from Ceylon.

The eyes of the watching Mohmands glistened as the Provindahs went past. Very soon those happy-go-lucky men would be forced to disgorge their wealth.

Camels followed laden with tight-curled, newly-cured lambskins from Astrakhan, beautiful things destined for the coats of rich merchants or the collars of fine ladies in the Western hemisphere. The camels made bubbling, grumbling noises as they went along on their curious, spongy-looking feet, their pannier loads swaying as if any moment they would roll off into the dust of the road.

Ten flat-faced Uzbegs on sturdy Kabuli ponies followed. They were on their way to Mecca, via the port of Karachi. Without a well-lined purse a man cannot travel to Medina to visit the tomb of the Prophet.

Bill Night glanced sympathetically at them. Unless he could do something, those Uzbegs would never walk seven times round the Kaaba in Mecca, kiss the holy stone, drink the waters of the Zemzem, and finally return to wear the green turban, and proudly proclaim themselves to be *Hadjis*—holy men. They were more likely to return dejected and penniless to their homes in far-off Khokand.

At each interval of fifty paces two more Mohmands wheeled their ponies and walked them alongside the dusty caravan. When the end came in sight Bill and Clay turned their own mounts and played their part. The other caravan guards were laughing and joking, but Bill Night was grim. He was trying to think of some way in which this caravan could be stopped without too many bullets flying. If the troops were called out of Landi Kotal the disguised Mohmands would fight. They were well armed, and men would die quickly when hot lead began to whine from the carbine muzzles.

The caravan poured up the steep incline. All too soon the glimmering white of the buildings at Landi Kotal came in sight. The flag still drooped idly in the hot air. The sentries watched from their shelters, and all was calm and quiet. By this time the sun was at its highest, and the heat was terrific. Dust-devils rose and whirled from the feet of man and beast. Horses snorted, trying to clear their nostrils. Men cursed as they wiped their lips. The dust was everywhere.

An old Pathan fell out of the caravan and sat down to rub his aching feet. Sight of him gave Bill an idea. He had just passed the last of the military buildings, but was near enough to be seen by the sentry on duty there.

Reeling, he pretended to struggle to keep his seat, while his pony pranced excitedly at the unexpected movement. Then like a man smitten by the sun, Bill toppled out of the saddle ; taking good care that his feet did not catch in the stirrups, he sprawled full length in the dust.

His pony, startled, threw up its heels and bolted down the line, causing men to hurriedly draw in out of the way. For some moments there was confusion. Clay Armstrong forced his pony through the ranks of the caravan and bent anxiously over his chief. Bill winked at him, then closed his eyes again, for the sound of galloping hooves told him some of the Mohmands were coming up.

" He has had a fit, or something," Clay Armstrong said, while Bill wriggled and squirmed in the dust.

" A thousand curses on him," snarled the Mohmand chief who was bringing up the rear. " What can we do with him ? Sling him across his saddle."

" Would a Sikh do that ? " Clay asked. " We must be careful not to arouse suspicion among the Feringhis. They will be watching."

" What, then, can we do, fool ? "

" Take him to the fort," Clay suggested. " What does one man matter where the plans of the Mullah are concerned ? If he dies because of the raid, well, will he not go to Paradise, and live there with the fruit of two gardens within easy reach, attended by Houris ? He will have his reward."

The Mohmand grunted. The caravan was moving away from them. Heat-stroke in the Khyber was not uncommon, and the British have even erected " heat-stroke " huts, where a man so afflicted may rest until the cool of evening. In that baking wilderness even men who have lived all their lives in the heat of India occasionally succumb in this way.

" Do thou take him to the fort, then, if that is the best way to allay suspicion," commanded the Mohmand, " and rejoin us as soon as possible."

" That I will," Clay retorted. " I have no wish to dally under the guns of the Feringhis.

The Mohmand chief allowed himself a grim smile. British justice was short and to the point. Raiders could expect only one end if they were caught.

" Allah go with thee, then," he said, mounting his pony. " Knowest thou where the caravan will leave the Pass ? "

" Does the Mullah tell me his plans ? " asked Clay. " Where shall I join you again, in case I am delayed ? "

" Take the nullah which leads up to Michni Gana," was the prompt reply. " In the hills behind we plan to loot the caravan, then send it empty on its way."

Clay nodded, and as the disguised Mohmand mounted his pony and galloped after the disappearing caravan, he lifted Bill across his own pony. The sentry eyed them curiously as they approached, but did not relax his vigilance. Men die too easily in the Khyber when they forget to take care, and even men in the uniform of the Sikhs may not be all they appear on the surface.

"Fetch the commandant immediately," Clay called out.

Bill was still lying across the saddle ; for all he knew, one of the Mohmands might have been detailed to watch and report what happened.

"Halt ! " was the sentry's reply. Then he yelled : "Turn out the guard ! "

"Don't waste time," snapped Clay. "We're British Secret Service, and there's trouble brewing."

"My aunt was the Queen of Sheba," the soldier snorted. "You stand where you are, cully ; I'm loaded with ball ammunition."

Clay subsided. He knew the sentry was doing his duty ; it was galling to waste time like this, but argument was useless.

Three minutes later, surrounded by perspiring soldiers, Bill and he were escorted into a room and searched. Their arms were taken away, and the officer of the guard, anything but pleased at being dragged out of a comparatively cool room, was listening to Bill with wide-open eyes.

" That detachment of Sikhs which took the caravan through are Mohmand tribesmen," Bill snapped, " and unless you look slippy they'll strip every mule, donkey, and camel, and India will ring with the news of it. The Mullah will have more followers than he'll know what to do with at the end of a week."

The officer of the guard scratched his chin dubiously. These two blue-eyed men in their Sikh uniform puzzled him.

" Sit down—I'll see the commandant," he snapped. As he reached the door he threw another sentence over his shoulder: "Heaven help you if you've been lying."

Bill merely grunted, then turned and begged a cigarette from the sergeant of the guard.

" A-a-ah ! " Bill sighed as he sucked at his cigarette. " A pipe is the best smoke of all, but a cig isn't at all bad when you haven't touched tobacco for several days."

The sergeant grinned.

" An inch o' thick twist, an' old clay pipe, an' if I can get my feet up on a table, I'm as happy as a bee in clover," he said. " Not that there are any blinkin' bees in this condemned hole. It's hotter . . ."

He shut his mouth like a trap as the commandant entered.

Bill rose easily and saluted. The commandant's eyes bulged as Bill addressed him by name. Before the commandant could speak he was listening to information which proved conclusively that Bill was William D. Night, Secret Service Agent. He listened silently to the story of the morning's happenings in the Pass, of the sending back of the Khassadars, and the tapping of the telephone wire. Then he turned to the officer of the guard standing behind his chair.

" Sound the ' alarm,' sir," he snapped. " We'll soon lay these rogues by the heels. Sergeant, send for the wireless operator. If the telephone wire has been tapped we must use wireless."

" Wait a minute, sir," Bill butted in. " I'd like to make one or two suggestions. If you follow now there'll be a fight, and a lot of the caravan people will be killed."

The commandant stiffened.

" Well, sir, what else can we do ? We can't let the raiders get away with the spoil."

He bristled with indignation at the thought.

Bill suppressed a smile.

" No, sir, of course not," he said, and tossed away the butt of his cigarette. " My idea is that you allow the Mohmands to rob the caravan. They'll send the caravaneers back to the Pass. Then we can put our spoke in. I suggest you get a couple of bombing 'planes sent out from Peshawar. They can hold the top of the Michni Gana valley, and your troops can come up from the Khyber Pass end . . . and it'll be a straight fight then, with no risk to the non-combatant caravan people. The Mohmands won't put up much of a fight, especially if the bombers drop a curtain of tear-gas bombs as a kind of peaceful persuader, before using high explosive."

The commandant tapped a tattoo with his finger ends. Then he rose.

" I'll see what Peshawar says," he grumbled. " I don't like this diplomacy with tribesmen. The only thing they understand is bullets and cold steel."

Bill nodded. He understood what was going through the soldier's mind. The commandant of Landi Kotal did not care too much for the idea of taking his men into the Michni Gana hills ; he would have preferred a running fight from the Khyber Pass. Bill, however, was thinking of the traders. If the British force from Landi Kotal attacked the disguised Mohmand raiders while they were with the caravan, men and beasts would be killed indiscriminately, and most of the raiders would probably get away.

Ten long minutes passed. Bill was beginning to grow impatient. Every minute counted, for he wanted to rejoin the Mohmands before the troops attacked, to be with them when they scattered and hurried back to the Mullah's hidden headquarters. Until the Mullah was captured or killed there would be no peace or security in the Khyber hills.

At length the commandant returned.

"The bombers will leave Peshawar in one hour's time," he said tersely. "We will follow you to the Michni Gana nullah at the same hour. I don't like the scheme—there's too much risk of their getting away—but Peshawar seems to have faith in your judgment, so the blame, if any, won't fall on me."

"Thank you, sir," said Bill, rising. "I don't think anything will go wrong. The fellow who told me the Mohmands would leave the Pass by the nullah which leads into Michni Gana had no reason to suspect I was a Britisher."

The commandant held out his hand. There was grudging admiration in his voice when he spoke.

"Well, Night, I think you're a dam' fool for going back among that gang of cut-throats," he growled. "Best of luck. I wouldn't do your job for ten times the salary."

" Thank you, sir," Bill said, taking the soldier's hand. " Somebody has to do it or the Border wouldn't be safe for any one. And it isn't really as dangerous as it seems. Clay and I have been doing it for eighteen months, and we're still alive and kicking."

" I can see that," the commandant grunted, " but you know the old maxim about taking the pitcher to the well once too often."

" Crikey, sir," Clay put in, " you'll have me going into a hot sweat if you keep talking like that."

The commandant smiled and offered them a drink, which was gratefully accepted. Five minutes later, with Bill on a borrowed pony, the two Secret Service men clattered out of the compound and into the heat and dust of the Pass.

They looked like two ordinary Sikh lancers, except that Bill had no lance with him now, only a carbine in its leather bucket. Down the slope from Landi Kotal they clattered, and finally reached the nullah which led off the Pass road to the Michni Gana hills.

The clip-clop of hoofs changed to a dull drumming as they left the metalled road and struck out over the sun-scorched grass. Their speed rapidly decreased, for the nullah rose swiftly. At the end of fifty minutes riding up the nullah, Bill reined in his panting pony. There was a frown on his face.

" Anything strike you, Clay ? " he asked.

Clay Armstrong flicked the beads of perspiration from his brow with his thumb nail.

" Yes," he said. " Five hundred camels, and as many donkeys, can't come up here without leaving some trace of their passing. I've been looking for camel dung this past ten minutes, and haven't seen a speck."

" Great minds think alike," Bill said grimly. " Either the Mohmand who told us the caravan would be taken up this nullah to the Michni Gana suspected us, or else Orlof has made a lightning change of plan. If we don't do something quickly the commandant's fears will be realized, and the raiders will get away with the richest loot for years."

" But the 'planes will spot them, surely," Clay protested. " They'll be able to see 'em as easy as winking from the air."

" I know that," said Bill. " But if the soldiers from Landi Kotal come up this nullah to the Michni Gana hills, and the caravan is in another valley, nothing on earth can stop the Mohmands from looting the caravan and getting away with the stuff. It'll be dark in another couple of hours."

Clay shrugged his shoulders.

" Well, what can we do ? " he asked. " If we don't know where the Mohmands are . . . we're helpless."

" Not quite," Bill assured him. " The soldiers from Landi Kotal won't turn out without portable wireless, in case they get in a jam. We've got to rush back to the Pass, contact the soldiers, and get them to wireless to the 'planes. It may mean a delay, possibly a scrap in the dark, which I don't like at all ; but it's better than Orlof and his men getting away scot free."

Clay wheeled his pony. Bill remounted, and they began the descent of the nullah. Neither pony had taken more than a dozen steps when a rifle cracked somewhere on the hillside. Bill ducked as a bullet droned viciously past his head. The rifle cracked again as Clay dug his heels into his pony's ribs ; the pony screamed as a bullet took it in the chest, then reared on its hind legs and teetered for a moment, giving Clay a chance to scramble hurriedly out of the saddle. Then the pony was kicking out its life on the ground.

Bill took his carbine gingerly out of its bucket and threw the weapon from him. He knew the wizardry of the hillmen with a rifle, and he did not wish to drop kicking like the pony. The only thing to do was to

86

surrender ; there was no means of telling whether they were ambushed by one rifleman or a score.

" Put up your hands ! "

The cry came from a spot about seventy yards away, where a gnarled outcrop of rock gave admirable cover for a sniper. Bill raised his hands. Clay did likewise, and a moment later a man came from behind the rock ; another showed himself, rifle in hand, as a hint that the first sign of treachery would be met with a bullet.

Clay crooned the first line of a song : " *When you come to the end of a perfect day . . .* "

" That's right, look on the bright side," murmured Bill. " If we get out of this alive, I'll be surprised, *and* we'll get the hide tanned off us. The Mohmands are going to get away with the loot as easy as winking. We've been duped."

He said no more, for the advancing tribesman, dressed as a Sikh lancer, was now only a few yards away.

CHAPTER SIX

IN the valley next but one to the Michni Gana there was considerable activity. Orlof had led the caravan aside from the Khyber Pass road, intimating to the leading Provindahs that ahead, in the Ali Masjid Gorge, there was an armed force which the British troops were even then trying to dislodge. A detour through the hills to Michni Fort on the Kabul River was necessary, and the caravan would spend the night there.

The Provindahs made little fuss. They all knew John Staines, who collected the Pass dues from them for distribution to the tribes. Payment of those dues guaranteed them from attack, and none of them suspected that the tall broad-shouldered Orlof was not the Political Agent.

Up a stony dry river bed they went, the camels protesting at their labour in the terrific heat. By the time that the tail of the long train of men and beasts had left the road, its head was entering a narrow valley whose yellow walls rose almost perpendicular for several hundred feet. It was an ideal place for the looting of a caravan.

When the whole concourse was in the narrow gorge the disguised Mohmands gathered the men of the caravan together. The lances were still in their buckets, but the wicked-looking carbines were now very much in evidence. The camel men, the Provindahs, and the other carriers noted this with increasing uneasiness. Hands strayed to guns, knives, hidden revolvers, only to come away again as the grim Mohmands edged closer, every man holding his carbine.

Orlof addressed the concourse.

" For years," be began, " ye have come through the Khyber to Peshawar from the land of the Amir, or from India to Afghanistan and beyond. A small payment has assured safe conduct through the Pass, and the heavy burden has been borne by the British Raj. The white man is no longer content to bear that burden ; to-day, he commandeers the merchandise in this caravan as an instalment of the tribute due to him for your many years of peaceful trading."

A gasp of mingled horror and amazement went up from the throng. These men might spit at mention of the British Raj, and hope that one day the British would be driven into the sea ; yet at the back of their minds the traders knew that only the strength of British rule kept peace along the Border. It was hard to believe that the British would descend to such barefaced robbery.

One old Provindah spoke up. In his tattered wallet reposed six pearls from the Gulf of Persia. In a Kashmir bazaar he hoped to make much profit from those six glistening baubles. He was terror-stricken at the thought that they would be taken from him.

"Lord, this is indeed a wicked thing which thou tellest us," he began. "Before to-day we have always said, though thieves shall steal upon us in Afghanistan, though robbers shall waylay us in the land of the Shah, in India we are safe. Will the mighty British turn loose-wallah? Shall the good name of a hundred years be ground into the dust for the poor stuff we carry with us? If it be so, the name of the white man will stink in the nostrils of all honest men for ever."

Orlof smiled at the speaker. The Mullah wished to rouse the anger of trader, hillman, and Hindu alike. The wealth of this caravan was not small, but it was more important to destroy the merchants' belief in the honesty of the rulers of India. Orlof's retort was edged with derision.

"O man who pretends to be poor, but who carries wealth such as a prince might envy," Orlof retorted, "the British have behaved too long as dotering fathers to such as you are. Shall a man continue to care for the dog which bites him ? Now the whip has been taken from its hook in the threshing shed. The white man's kindness is ended. Will that satisfy thee, old man ? "

The Provindah had gone pale at the reference to the wealth he carried. He opened his mouth to speak, and decided that words were no longer of use. A low murmur of indignation ran through the crowd. Had there been a leader among them they might even then have struck a blow in defence of their property, but there was no such leader. Before they could gather their scattered wits Orlof gave an order.

" Camel drivers, unload your merchandise. Donkey men, do the same." With a wave of his hand he indicated the old Provindah : " Such as you, old man, who carry your merchandise in a wallet, will come over on my left hand. My Sikh lancers will attend to ye."

For a moment it seemed as if the merchants would fight. The haughty, flat-faced Uzbegs, who could see ahead of them an ignominious return to Khokand, murmured among themselves, and there was a general tightening up of faces.

The Sikhs threw off the safety-catches of their

carbines. For a moment the issue hung in the balance. Orlof's face had lost its sneering grin. He had not anticipated resistance.

Then a little Pathan boy, slung in a basket on the back of a camel, began to whimper ; instinctively eyes were turned that way, and the moment of mounting courage passed. The menacing muzzles of the carbines curbed the anger of the stoutest hearted, and in sullen silence the unloading began.

When the task was half accomplished a persistent buzzing from the cloudless sky drew the attention of Mohmand and trader alike. The high walls of the narrow valley gave a restricted view of the heavens ; the buzzing grew louder, faded again, and swelled to a roar as a big three-engined bombing 'plane sailed into view, and turned to follow swiftly the full length of the valley.

Orlof stared, his face paling a little. Was this just coincidence, or had news of the outrage leaked out in some miraculous way ?

The bomber turned again and again, coming lower and lower as it drove along the valley. The hopes of the traders were aroused, while the curses of the disguised Mohmands increased in intensity.

The 'plane finally went off, and as it did so a bunch

of horsemen appeared at the lower end of the valley. They comprised six men who had been watching the Michni Gana hills, with their two prisoners, Bill Night and Clay Armstrong.

Bill and Clay were both astride one pony, and the poor beast was almost exhausted. Bill Night weighed over thirteen stones, and Clay was only a little lighter.

Under the keen eyes of their guards Bill urged the pony across to where Orlof watched his men compel the Provindahs to hand over their wealth. The merchants were wailing and pleading for mercy; Orlof, cold and cynical, sneered at the old men and threatened the young ones.

Bill Night slid off the panting pony, and bowing low before Orlof he asked:

"Lord, must I be treated like a felon because I fainted in the Pass?" Bill put all the injured innocence into his voice he was capable of. "We came from the fort at Landi Kotal, having borrowed a pony, and entered the Michni Gana valley, as we were told to do by the men who rode last of all your troop. Seeing no sign of the caravan, we turned to go back to the Pass, hoping to pick up the trail; and at once we were made prisoners, my cousin having his pony shot under him."

Orlof looked at Bill.

"It seems strange," he gibed, "that one who has travelled the Border country should be smitten with the heat at the Landi Kotal fort. And thy cousin, I was told, was over keen to risk his neck in carrying thee into the very lion's mouth."

Turning to the men who had captured Bill and Clay, he snapped out an order.

"Bind them. I think we shall have a pleasant evening making these two spies talk."

For a moment Bill toyed with the idea of grabbing Orlof and holding him as a hostage. He knew the Mohmands would not dare fire if there was a risk of hitting their leader. Bill put the idea away, however. He shrugged his shoulders.

"As my lord wishes," he said simply. "I would only ask him to remember by whom he was rescued from the Malik Din Khels."

A sneer was Orlof's only response; and a moment later the Mohmand guards were picking up rope cut from the bulky camel packs.

Before they could start trussing-up the two Secret Service men, however, the bomber reappeared. It sailed serenely along the valley from the west; and when it passed above the huddled crowd of men and beasts, several small objects were released, to fall swiftly earthwards.

All eyes had been directed to the 'plane, and there was an immediate scattering as the bombs fell. Disguised Mohmands and traders alike did their best to get as far away from the spot where it seemed the bombs would fall.

Bill and Clay took the opportunity of mixing with the squealing, grunting camels. They knew that the bombs would be not high explosive, but tear-gas.

" Thank goodness there's no wind to-day," Clay gasped, as he dexterously avoided a bite from a snarling camel. " That gas will hang in this rotten valley for an hour or more."

With sounds like the bursting of electric light bulbs the bombs exploded, and a chorus of jeers greeted the noises. The Mohmands knew the effect of high explosive, and they thought the lack of noise denoted poor bombs. Anxiously they watched the 'plane as it roared out of sight. The hum of the triple engines grew less ; but as the Mohmands were beginning to sort themselves out again, and round up the merchants, another 'plane appeared. It passed over, and dropped four bombs ; then the first 'plane reappeared.

For forty minutes, while shadows began to deepen

in the valley, this went on. The work of robbing the caravan was held up, for the Mohmands could never be certain where the next bombs would fall, or whether they too, like the predecessors, would be " duds."

Then the gas began to seep down the valley as the heat subsided. A Mohmand blinked, muttered to himself, and then wiped his eyes. Others were afflicted in the same way. In five minutes half the crowd were blinking and cursing as they tried to dry their tears.

The owners of camels and donkeys took the halters off their beasts, and gathering as much of their merchandise as they could, loaded it into the panniers ; the Mohmands strode about, cursing and threatening, unable to do anything for the tears which blinded them.

The camels began to feel the effects of the gas, and soon there was a general retreat down the valley in the direction of the Khyber Pass. Scattered about in heaps were bundles of valuable Astrakhan pelts, splendid hand-worked rugs from Bokhara, and bales of beautiful silks from Herat.

The Mohmand raiders seemed to loose all interest in loot. They rode their ponies down the valley, and after travelling a couple of hundred yards found their tears beginning to dry up. They were out of the gas zone, and very soon recovered their sight.

The caravan men did not pause when they found their tears ceasing. They wanted to get down to the comparative security of the Khyber Pass. The valley echoed with the shouts of the Mohmands ordering the merchants to halt. Rifles crackled, and camels fell sprawling in the dust. The headlong retreat stopped.

Orlof, wiping his eyes, was almost beside himself with rage. He bellowed commands, and very soon his men were gathered about him. A score of them held up the advance of the terrified merchants.

" Gather what goods ye can," he shouted. " Then we will go down the valley until we find a spot where we can lead our horses over into the Michni Gana. Someone has betrayed . . ."

He did not finish the sentence, for a hawk-eyed Mohmand had seen the vanguard of the British force from Landi Kotal fort, and he gave tongue immediately.

In front of the main body of soldiers came Bren-gunners. They did not fire, but dodged from cover to cover, waiting for the first shot to be fired by the Mohmands.

The merchants, being men of resource, flung themselves flat on the ground, as far away from the

Mohmands as possible. The latter, shaken by the sudden appearance of the troops, and not yet recovered from their fright with the gas, did not think of using the merchants as hostages, but immediately sought cover and began to fire.

The Bren-gunners did not reply, but made themselves secure in positions from which they could sweep the valley when necessary. It seemed that the rapidly-gathering gloom would allow the Mohmands to leave their ponies and scramble to safety up the steep sides of the valley.

But the two bombing 'planes reappeared, roaring above the valley. With magnificent aiming, their crews dropped bombs which exploded just behind the tribesmen. The latter, risking a blast of bullets, jumped to their feet and scurried a few yards nearer to the troops.

Then the gas began to make itself felt again. The Mohmands cursed, tried to hold their breath, tried to cover their eyes, but the insidious vapour penetrated everything, and soon they were forced to rise and seek the purer air lower down the valley.

Bill and Clay wormed across to Orlof, who was spluttering and cursing. Bill had a mission to perform, and he intended to finish his job, even if it meant temporarily keeping Orlof out of the hands of the troops.

" Lord," he gasped, for the tear-gas was spreading quickly. " If we rush up the valley we may be able to escape."

Orlof seized on the idea as a drowning man will clutch at the proverbial straw. Stumbling like drunken men they went into the gas, heading up the valley. A few of the Mohmands who saw them followed, but the majority were already within easy range of the Bren-gunners, and throwing down their arms.

Over came the 'planes again. A bomb dropped ten yards ahead of the stumbling trio. A wave of gas hit them like a blow, but they fought their way through. Tears were streaming down their faces, their eyes were swollen until it was almost impossible to see anything ahead. The exposed parts, damp with perspiration, smarted wickedly under the influence of the gas, and by the time they staggered into comparatively pure air they were exhausted.

Regardless of the rough screes they dropped like logs, and lay breathing in gasping sobs. Bill and Clay at the end of ten minutes began to chew the ends of their turbans to induce some saliva to come into their mouths. Three of the Mohmands who had followed their leader were doing likewise. Orlof was cursing in a husky undertone, almost beside himself with chagrin at the last-minute defeat of his project.

The shadows deepened in the narrow valley. The blue sky turned almost purple, with wonderful little wisps of cloud blood-red above the setting sun. The six weary figures made a vague splash of white in a slowly darkening background.

Bill thought hard while recovering from the effects of the gas. He was tempted to make Orlof a prisoner, and so to remove one very dangerous lieutenant of the Mullah. But before he showed his hand Bill meant to find out where the real John Staines was hidden. For this reason Clay and he must accompany Orlof back to the cave of the Mullah.

Having made his decision Bill touched Orlof on the shoulder.

" Lord," he said humbly, " would it not be wiser if we left this valley ? The accursed Feringhis may decide to search for us . . . and we are in no fit state to scatter like sheep out of their way."

Orlof raised a swollen face. His eyes were mere slits, and much of his resemblance to John Staines had vanished. Bill noticed with something of a shock that the other's moustache was a fake. It hung awry, loosened either by salt tears or by Orlof's clawing at his face.

Looking for a moment at the five men with him, Orlof sighed deeply. Then a bitter smile crossed his face.

"Thanks to thee, friend," he said to Bill, "I am not a prisoner. Thou shalt be remembered when I tell the tale of this day to the Mullah."

"May thy shadow increase," Bill murmured.

"Come, let us climb," grunted Orlof as he struggled to his feet. "This set-back will mean little to the Mullah."

In silence the six men began to scramble over the sharp rocks. Clay Armstrong caught Bill's eye and lifted his own eyebrows significantly, as if to ask: "Haven't we done enough for the time being?"

Bill understood that look. He grinned, and jerked a finger to indicate that they must go ahead. There was still work to be done.

CHAPTER SEVEN

BILL and Clay were never likely to forget that nightmare journey from the top of the valley over the Michni Gana hills to the Mullah's headquarters. The day had started very early for them, the only food they had eaten had been their hurried breakfast ; when the excitement of the attack and the discomfort of the gas had faded a little, the party found themselves parched with thirst and ready to drop in their tracks from fatigue.

Bill Night was tough, Clay was in the pink of condition, they were both accustomed to walking about these danger-infested hills under all conditions ; but never had either known such weariness.

When the first pink rays showed in the eastern sky they came upon a solitary little hut, where an old Shinwari goatherd was allowed to live in peace because he was unarmed and had nothing worth stealing.

The bleating of goats attracted the attention of the party, and they turned aside. Ten minutes later the trembling goatherd was watching his goats being milked. Bill would have liked to toss the old man a coin in payment; but a tough Pathan would never do such a thing, and he was forced to laugh with the others at the piteous figure of the old man deprived of his breakfast. They left him bowing to them, and muttering curses under his breath.

The sun was almost overhead when they finally reached the Mullah's cave. The Mohmands on guard at the cave stared incredulously at the remnant of the proud band of looters who had started out thirty hours before.

There was a pregnant silence as the six weary men paused. Orlof waved his hand.

"Be seated. In a moment your wants will be attended to."

Bill and Clay did not need to act relief at being able to totter into the shade and stretch their bodies on the ground. Orlof staggered into the darkness of the cave; the other Mohmands gathered round, demanding to know what had happened.

Bill and Clay allowed their companions to relate the terrors of the previous afternoon. Eyes narrowed, men fingered their guns, as they heard how the loot had been snatched from the hands of the raiding party almost at the moment when they were ready to load it on to the saddles of the ponies.

"By the beard of the Prophet," one swarthy Mohmand snarled. "The Mullah promised us the loot of India, and yet his plan to rob the caravan fails miserably, and all our comrades, save ye five, are carried off, maybe to hang outside the walls of Peshawar."

"Speak softly," Bill cautioned, for he had seen out of the corner of his eye that Orlof had paused on his way out of the cave to listen to the conversation. Bill wanted to convince the man that he was whole-heartedly for the Mullah. "Speak softly," he repeated, "for a wise man keeps a still tongue when fools babble. Shall we wail because an eagle takes one sheep from the flock? Are there not three score other sheep . . . and will there not be more after lambing time. The Mullah is all-wise. He will make the accursed Feringhis pay."

"Can the Mullah bring back my son, who yesterday rode out so gaily in Sikh uniform?" demanded one grizzled warrior.

"If thy son dies," Bill countered, "will he not sit in Paradise, with ten beautiful houris to bring him cooling drinks and fruit from lovely gardens? Great will be the rewards of those who are faithful to the Mullah. . . ."

"Spoken like a warrior," Orlof growled as he came out of the shadows. "The Mullah will know how to reward such as thee."

Bill bowed, hiding the twinkle in his eyes. His defence of the Mullah might stand him in good stead in the future. How useful his words had been he was very shortly to realize, for Orlof commanded the five of them to follow him into the cave.

In the brilliantly lighted inner chamber they faced the swarthy Mullah. His green silken turban glistened like some giant emerald in the strong light. He stroked his well trimmed beard as if in calm meditation, but his eyes betrayed the anger he felt at the bad news Orlof had brought him.

"Ye five have shown yourselves to be men of courage," he began, as Bill and the others bowed low. "Your reward shall be great. I am pleased with what ye did . . . and as a sign of my pleasure I am giving ye a chosen task."

He paused and looked at the men before him, and Bill Night fancied there was a cynical twist to the cruel mouth. After a pause the Mullah continued.

"We have with us, in another cave, one who is valued highly by the British Raj. He is the man who has made himself, as he calls it, a friend of the tribesmen during the past three years. Ye may not know him by name . . . but the white men call him John Staines."

Bill was conscious of a sinking feeling in his stomach; something most unpleasant was coming. The premonition was borne out a moment later. The Mullah made a signal to a Mohmand standing by the heavy curtains which apparently masked the entrance to another cave. The Mohmand bowed himself out through the curtains, and the Mullah resumed his speech.

" This John Staines is an enemy. Our friend Orlof is able to make himself very much like this Staines . . . and through his cleverness we shall accomplish a great deal."

The Mullah rubbed his hands together softly and went on.

" Since we cannot have two Political Agents in the Khyber, one must die."

He shot a keen glance first at Bill Night, and then at Clay Armstrong. Neither moved a muscle.

At that moment the curtains parted, and into the cave walked John Staines. The Political Agent's face was haggard, but his cold blue eyes were unchanged, and the proud set of his shoulders indicated that his imprisonment had not affected his courage.

"Quite a party, I see," he said coolly; "with myself, I presume, as the honoured guest."

"Very honoured," the Mullah replied acidly. "These five men have proved their courage and cleverness by escaping from a force of men sent from Landi Kotal, aided by bombing 'planes and gas. Not even all the might of the British Raj can defeat the hillman when he has right on his side."

Staines looked at the five men. Each bore grim evidence of the ordeal of the previous day. The smart Sikh uniforms with which they had been equipped were torn and stained, and their faces were still swollen.

Staines laughed insolently.

"Well," he drawled, "they look as if they had a rough time proving their courage and cleverness. I don't suppose they'll be eager to pit themselves against British soldiers again in a hurry."

The Mullah half rose, his face a mask of hate.

"Thy tongue will shortly lose its sting, my friend," he snarled. "I reward these men in a way they will enjoy. Quite a party, as thou hast said; they are the party—the firing party."

Staines paled, and lifted his chin; his laugh was the laugh of a man without a care in the world.

"My friend, a man can die but once," he retorted,

" and I would rather die thus, in the service of my country, than dangle at the end of a rope, as you most surely will do. Release me, and I'll promise to do what I can for you. If you have a legitimate grievance I'll see it is remedied. If you don't care to do that— well, as surely as my name is John Staines, there's a rope in some army stores at Peshawar that'll cling lovingly to your neck before many days are over."

The Mullah had recovered his poise, and he laughed.

" Spoken like a man," he said. " Thou, and I too, can die whether by bullet or by rope. Nevertheless, I do not think a Peshawar rope will cling lovingly to *my* neck."

He turned to Orlof.

" Issue these men with loaded rifles, and mark off twelve paces in the outer cavern. The execution will take place at once."

Bill Armstrong looked across at Staines. The man had suffered, there was no doubt about that. There was a half-healed scar on his neck, as if some one had attempted to knife him. His usually smooth chin was now bristly and unkempt. His face was leaner, and dirty. But his eyes were alight with a fine pure courage.

Staines, who could probably have been a successful

business man, had dedicated his life to his country. He had come out to India to serve the interests of Briton and Hindu. His later career had been devoted to solving the many delicate problems of the Border. He had endeavoured to keep the peace in the Khyber, risking his life many times as he did so. And now he was to die in a dark cave up in the hills where he had done his best work.

Bill weighed the matter as coolly as it was possible. He and Clay could try and save John Staines. There was one chance in ten thousand that sudden action might be successful. It was almost certain that all three of them would be shot in the attempt, or would stand together to face a firing squad a few minutes later.

Bill asked himself what Staines would ask them to do if he was aware of their identity; and at once he knew the answer. Staines would want them to keep their secret, and continue to work for the undoing of the Mullah. Better one British Political Agent shot dead in the gloom of a cave than a war which might cost the lives of hundreds.

" We've got to go through with it, that's all," Bill thought, and registered a vow that if John Staines died, the Mullah would very soon follow him to the grave.

A few moments later Orlof appeared and nodded. The Mullah rose from his seat, and spread a hand towards the outer cave.

"We are ready, John Staines," he said mockingly. "Hast thou any last wish to be fulfilled?"

"Nothing you could do, thanks," said the Political Agent. "I've let a mangy cur lick my hand, because it wanted to thank me for food. But I accept nothing from a vulture like you. When the tribesmen have paid the price for following you, they'll realize what you are—a pariah dog."

"Brave words," was the sneering answer. "We'll see if you can talk like that when the rifles are pointed at your fine chest."

As they walked through into the outer cave Clay Armstrong moved to Bill's side.

"What are we doing, sir?" he asked.

Bill had time for one whispered sentence.

"He wouldn't thank us for trying to save him if it lost us our chance of dishing the Mullah."

Clay gulped. This was going to be one of the hardest tasks of all his Secret Service.

The Political Agent was stood against the cave wall. One of the brilliant lights was brought in from the Mullah's chamber. The firing party was lined up.

The Mullah asked him if he would like his eyes bandaged.

III

The faces of the three Mohmands were grim ; it was a feat of marksmanship to kill a man from a mountain crest, but to shoot him from twelve paces was not a good thing to do, especially when the man was brave and taunted his captors to the last.

Bill and Clay were perspiring as the rifles were handed to them. Clay cast a last agonized glance at his chief, but Bill was staring grimly at Staines, and Staines was quite calm.

The Mullah asked him if he would like his eyes bandaged. A smile and a shake of the head was the reply. Orlof pinned a small square of paper on the left breast of the condemned man, and then stood back.

" When I count four," said the Mullah, " you will fire at the white mark. I want to see just one hole in that paper. Mohmands are capital marksmen. Let me see you at your best."

The rifles were lifted. The Mullah began to count. He counted slowly, deliberately, as if wishing to prolong the mental agony of Staines.

" One . . . two . . . three . . . Four ! "

He shouted the last word, and the five rifles belched flame and smoke.

CHAPTER EIGHT

THROUGH the stinging cordite smoke the five members of the firing party were amazed to see John Staines still standing erect. His face was deathly pale, and beads of sweat stood on his forehead.

Bill Night knew himself not far from collapse ; by a great effort of will he resumed his usual self-control. Even in his perilous work such an ordeal was, fortunately, exceptional.

A curt command from the Mullah, and John Staines was led away to the place whence he had come. Orlof told the firing party to ground their weapons, but offered no explanation as to why the Political Agent had not been killed. Bill and Clay had both aimed wide, but no doubt the other three members of the firing party had obeyed orders.

The rifles were collected by a six-feet-six Mohmand. Then Bill and Clay were escorted into the Mullah's room. With mixed feelings they faced the man again. He looked at them for a few seconds with a trace of a smile on his face.

"Be seated," he said curtly, indicating two chairs with a careless wave of his hand. Long training saved Bill and Clay from making a mistake which would have betrayed them. A Pathan never sits in a chair if he can help it. His natural method of resting is to squat on his haunches. The two Secret Service men sank down without a word, ignoring the chairs. Bill saw a look of understanding pass between the Mullah and Orlof.

"Ye may wonder," the Mullah said, "why my prisoner did not die when ye fired at him."

Bill shrugged his shoulders.

"The wisdom of the Mullah is beyond us," he murmured. "Who are we to say where a bullet shall go? It is as the Mullah decrees."

Clay, maintaining his rôle, was silent.

"The rifles were loaded with blank cartridge," the Mullah went on. "I wished to test your loyalty. Twice ye have done well ; ye rescued Orlof from the Malik Din Khels, and helped him out of the trap set by the British ; yet I am accustomed to make sure of men whom I trust. If ye would shoot down this Political Agent, then ye are not spies of the British."

Bill half rose, his eyes stormy.

"Lord——" he began, in the voice of a Pathan whose honour had been impugned.

The Mullah waved him down again with an imperious gesture.

"Enough. Now I trust ye. Go and eat. Rest, also, for to-morrow I give you charge of a band who will strike a mighty blow against the rule of the British in the Khyber."

Bill knew better than to open his mouth. He rose and left the inner cavern, with Clay at his heels. Outside they found food waiting for them, and when they had eaten they slept in the coolness of the outer cave.

An hour before sundown they were awakened by the sound of an aeroplane engine, and looking out saw what appeared to be a single-engined reconnaissance 'plane, with the red, white, and blue marking rings of the R.A.F. on its wings. The 'plane flew over the hills, dipping low over the villages, and once Bill thought he saw something drop through the hot air.

Next morning Bill was summoned to speak with the Mullah again. Orlof was not there. The Mullah's words were crisp and to the point.

"Forty men are waiting in the uniform of the Rajput regiment," he said. "Here are uniforms for thee and thy cousin. Don them at once. Thou wilt take thy men as quickly as possible to the heat-stroke hut at the top of the Ali Masjid Gorge. There thou wilt see Orlof, playing the part of John Staines the Political Agent. The headmen of the tribes have been summoned to a meeting. The 'plane which flew over yesterday belonged to me, and dropped messages, supposedly from the British. The meeting is to discuss the attempted looting of the caravan. Thy men will arrest all the headmen. Is that understood ? "

Bill quickly repeated the gist of the orders. Then asked :

" When the headmen have been arrested, what then, lord ? "

The Mullah smiled.

" Thou wilt see," he chuckled. " This day's work will undo much of what the British have done during the past ten years. Now go."

Bill went. He found uniforms of the proud Rajput regiment laid out for Clay and himself. Donning them, the pair joined the assembled tribesmen, all spick and span as Rajput soldiers.

The next two hours went quickly as the armed force made its way by goat track and rocky valley across to the Khyber. When they came out in the Pass above the Ali Masjid Gorge the sun was at full heat, though the time was only ten o'clock. One of the men crept to an eminence which overlooked the heat-stroke hut, and returned to say that the headmen of the tribes were already assembled, and that Orlof was addressing them in his rôle of Political Agent.

Forming his men into threes Bill took them down on to the hot Pass road. They crossed the military railway, and an engine-driver taking stores up to the camp at Landi Kotal waved a cheery greeting. Bill waved back, and wished with all his heart that he could have stopped the engine and sent a message to Landi Kotal for transference at speed to Peshawar. Instead he had to step briskly ahead with his men.

They reached the heat-stroke hut, a cool stone building erected by the British for the convenience of travellers overcome by the heat. In a ring twenty yards to the rear the headmen of a dozen tribes were seated ; listening to the impassioned tones of Orlof.

At a single word of command the men with Bill wheeled ; their rifles came up, and the seated tribesmen found themselves covered. Orlof moved out of the line of fire, shouting an order.

" Shoot down the first man who moves ! "

The dismayed headmen sat still, their countenances

as immobile as time-weathered stone. Then the headman of the Adam Khels rose slowly to his feet, having laid down his rifle as a sign that he meant to make no resistance.

"What is this trick?" he snarled. "Did we not come here at thy invitation, Staines Sahib, to discuss peace in the Pass?"

There was a low growl from the assembled headmen. For fifteen minutes Orlof, as John Staines, had been pleading for a better understanding between the tribes and the British Raj. He had promised all manner of concessions—and now he had cornered them.

Orlof laughed and spoke again.

"Listen, swine!" he began.

The eyes of the tribesmen bulged, for to them no insult was greater than to be likened to one of the hated unclean pig tribe. "The British are tired of trying to make peace with ye. Therefore the heads of every tribe will now go to prison and remain there as a hostage for a year. Unless peace in the Pass is maintained ye will all swing from the gallows."

A roar of rage went up from the unhappy headmen. Several reached for their rifles, only to draw back when the threatening weapons of the watchful "Rajputs" swung round.

" Is this, then, the honour of the white man ? " the headman of the Adam Khels asked in a choked voice.

" Stand back from your weapons," Orlof snapped. " I have wasted enough of my valuable time. In a few minutes lorries from Peshawar will come along this road, and ye will be taken where ye belong . . . behind stone walls."

The rifles were carefully collected, the headmen not daring to make a hostile move. Then the prisoners were formed into two ranks and marched into the Pass, the disguised Mohmands keeping them covered all the time.

At this point there was a sharp bend in the road. Rounding this Bill felt his hair rise on the nape of his neck as he saw before him two clumps of men, each behind a machine gun.

Then the voice of the Mullah rang out clear from behind a boulder.

" Let every man who wishes to live drop his weapons. If there is one gun above ground level when I count three the machine guns will speak."

The positions were reversed with a vengeance. The disguised Mohmands dropped their weapons. The headmen of the tribes, not too sure whether they were facing friends or foes, stood fast. Then from behind rocks on either side of the road came more of the Mullah's men. They quickly retrieved all the rifles, even the weapons which had belonged to the unhappy leaders of the tribes.

The whole body of men was ushered off the Pass road, and into a nullah which hid them from sight. Then the Mullah gave orders for the disguised Mohmands to be secured wrist to wrist, and when this was done he addressed the headmen of the various tribes.

" Friends, but for me ye would soon have been in prison. Ye see, now, what the British have in mind. The tribes are to be subdued. Your independence is to go. This white man, who for so long has persuaded you he was a friend, is shown as the snake he is. By a trick such as only a white man could contrive he would rob your tribes of their leaders." The Mullah paused to let his words sink deep. After a moment he went on :

" *La illa ha illalla Muhammad Rasilalah* [there is no God but Allah, and Mohammed is his Prophet]. Last night I saw a vision of the trick which this Political Agent tried to play on ye. To me in my dreams came the Irreproachable, the Pure in heart, the Greatest of the Great . . . Mohammed. To me in my dreams he said: 'From the hands of the accursed infidel rescue these warriors of mine, for they shall join with thee in a *Jehad* [a holy war] against the white man. With my help shall the infidel be swept into the sea ; the men of the hills shall plunder Hindustan, and the Pathan will walk in the land which rightly belongs to him.'"

The headmen were nodding their heads in agreement by the time the Mullah finished his impassioned speech. From the bazaars of Peshawar had trickled the news of this Mullah, and the great things he meant to do ; now they had evidence of his power.

The leader of the Adam Khels stood forward with flashing eyes, still enraged at what he thought to have been the work of the British.

" Great One," he said majestically, " I command eight hundred rifles. The Adam Khels are behind thee to a man. Speak the word, and bullets shall whistle a death song in the Khyber. Too long has the white man said ' yea ' to us, and we have done a thing, or ' nay,' and we have been still. If it is the will of Allah, then lead us on."

Others rose and said similar things. The eyes of the Mullah were bright with triumph. This stratagem had accomplished its object. The mock arrest by Orlof in the guise of John Staines had roused the anger of them all.

" Go back to your homes," the Mullah said. " I shall take these prisoners with me and deal with them as they deserve. To-morrow I will send word to you. The time is ripe for an attack on the forts, but *ye must work together*, as an army works, not in units as separate tribes."

At this last injunction several of the headmen glanced uneasily about them. Some of the tribes were in a state of armed truce, and only the urgency of the summons made by means of the aeroplane had brought their headmen together.

" In the name of Allah the Merciful and Magnificent," went on the Mullah, " I call on you to forget blood feuds for the time being. He who sheds the blood of a brother during the time of holy war shall never reach the paradise of the houris."

With that the Mullah stalked majestically up the nullah, followed by his Mohmands herding the men disguised as Rajput soldiers. There was little time lost in getting away from the scene, and the headmen of the various tribes quickly dispersed. The Pass was very quiet, but it might not remain so for long ; the safest place for a tribesman, when an assault had taken place on soldiers of the British Raj, was in the hills.

Once they were away from the scene of the mock ambush, the bonds were taken off Bill, Clay, and the men whom Bill had led. The Mullah and Orlof were in high spirits.

" Never was a neater trick played," chuckled Orlof. " Before sundown the story will have spread far—the story of how the Political Agent tried to dupe the headmen of the villages."

" It has been a good day," agreed the Mullah, taking the end of his green turban away from his mouth for a moment. " We have the tribes ready for revolt, and we must strike immediately. One good blow, while the poor fools we've just left try conclusions with the British Army, and we can leave this cursed country with enough wealth to last a couple of lifetimes."

When they finally reached the cave a surprise awaited the Mullah. In the inner cave waited the Semite from Merv, the dark-skinned, hook-nosed man whom Clay Armstrong had followed in the caravan going from Peshawar to the Afghan country, only to lose him somewhere in the Khyber Pass.

There was no bowing low to the Mullah by the Semite. His eyes flashed fire when he asked :

" What foolishness is this ? Two hundred Mohmand tribesmen captured by the troops from Landi Kotal ! There is trouble afoot. The British are preparing a punitive force against the Mohmands."

He spread his hands in anger, and went on.

" Have I been risking my life in Peshawar and beyond, so that thou canst make foolish mistakes ? The bazaars at Peshawar are crammed with valuables. The banks are reputed to contain twenty lakhs of rupees. Everything was ripe for our plan—and now the British are preparing."

The Mullah's eyes gleamed, not with anger, but with excitement.

" When do the British propose to enter the Pass ? " he asked.

" To-morrow," snarled the Semite, " and they will find the tribes only too willing to help. Half a dozen planes, and if the Mohmands try to resist they will be bombed out of existence.

The Mullah laughed.

" The tribes will not help the troops," he said. " I have played a trick on them to-day they will not easily forget."

He hurriedly outlined what had happened, and some of the anger faded from the Semite's flashing black eyes.

"Furthermore," the Mullah continued, "I wireless now to our amiable airman friend, and ask him to come across and drop a few small bombs on the villages through the Pass area. That will infuriate the tribes still further. They will be glad enough to fight on any pretext."

"But what about Peshawar?" the Semite persisted.

The Mullah nodded easily.

"I have that in mind, friend. I am not here merely to annoy the British. To-morrow morning, before sunrise, I shall skirt the Pass via Michni Fort, and be at the gates of the city by dusk. My men will be arrayed in Rajput uniform, and we shall gain entrance easily enough. The troops left to act as guards will be decoyed to the east by a sham attack, and we shall raid the banks at our leisure. Thy preparations are made?"

The Semite's eyes were now glistening with enthusiasm.

"The moment you wireless," he said, "my man in Peshawar will be ready. We cannot fail."

" We stand to make a quarter of a million," Orlof put in.

Turning to the powerful wireless set, he opened the cabinet and switched on the current, which was supplied by an amazing number of dry batteries.

" There'll be no police to trace this robbery," he added.

The Mullah seated himself before the instrument and began to rattle out a code call.

Meanwhile, sitting apart from the other men, Bill and Clay discussed in whispers a scheme for counteracting the Mullah's plans. They did not, of course, know that the authorities at Peshawar were preparing a punitive expedition to punish the Mohmands for their part in the attack on the caravan, but they did realize that things were coming to a head.

The sun set in a red glory behind the Safed Koh hills ; Bill and Clay sat watching the red deepen to a wondrous blood-flecked purple.

" As we can't possibly sneak away from here," Bill murmured, " we've got to take a chance on being able to use the Mullah's wireless set."

" If we're caught it'll mean a sticky sort of death," Clay said calmly ; " but there *is* a sporting chance of getting word through that way, and I can't see us being able to reach Fort Ali Masjid before dawn. So what odds? We've got to do something."

They waited patiently for darkness to cover the mountains. The sky went dark blue in the east, then deep purple. Night falls swiftly in that part of the world, but to the waiting Britishers it seemed to come with obstinate deliberation.

The evening meal was cooked and eaten. One by one the Mohmands began to roll themselves in their sheepskins. Four guards were selected to patrol the mouth of the cave. One tall tribesman stood at the entrance to the inner cave, and him Bill considered carefully. He would have to be very quietly disposed of if entrance to that inner cave was to be obtained.

Finally, with a last yawn, a man who had been trying to mend a shoe by the aid of a small lamp, put aside his work and lay down to sleep.

"These blighters don't seem to realize that one hour's sleep before midnight is worth two afterwards," Clay Armstrong whispered. "Isn't it just maddening to watch them?"

Bill grinned.

"You've said a mouthful, my lad. Now, what about our toss-up?"

He produced a rupee, shook it about in his big

hands, then turned one palm up. " What is it ? If you win you go into the inner cave. If not, I go."

" Head," murmured Clay.

Bill felt carefully at the coin for a moment, then he chuckled softly.

" You lose," he whispered.

Clay felt for Bill's hand and gripped it hard.

" Best of luck, sir," he muttered. " If you don't succeed, I'll do my best to get out. I've still got my ' plum ' bombs."

Bill returned the grip. Each knew that this was a gamble with death. Neither the Mullah nor Orlof had reappeared since they entered the inner cave late in the afternoon.

Clay lay down, clasping in each hand a tiny bomb. These weapons, about the size of a Victoria plum, were more likely to frighten an enemy than to harm him, although if they exploded near enough they could certainly do damage.

Bill rose quietly. He had wrapped rags round his spiked shoes. He felt his way along the cave wall.

A movement of the Mohmand who guarded the inner cave helped him in deciding where he was. His pulse was beating quickly, and although his brain was clear, as usual, the palms of his hands were moist.

Bill Night on a job was a cold and purposeful man, but just now, knowing what depended on him, he felt his nerves were a little on edge.

The raucous snoring all around was sufficient to drown any slight noise his feet might make on the cold floor of the cave. Bill was depending on those same snores to drown the noise of a blow.

He heard the man move restlessly. His rifle clinked as some metal portion touched the wall. Bill smiled, for the sound guided him. His muscles tightened ominously. Bill was a big man, and tough as whipcord. If he could just get a punch in at the right spot the Mohmand would take no further interest in proceedings for some time to come.

"If only his rifle drops backwards against the cave wall, it won't make too much clatter," thought Bill.

He breathed deeply, and as quietly as possible. He was a couple of yards from the man now, and the Mohmand seemed to have caught a sound of movement, for the rustle of his clothing ceased. He was obviously listening, wondering whether his ears were playing him false.

At that moment one of the tiny camel-dung fires emitted a spurt of blue flame. The little light showed

Bill to the Mohmand, and showed the Mohmand to Bill.

The Mohmand started to open his mouth, probably to cry out. Bill leaped, and his right fist, starting its course from just behind his hip, caught the guard a terrific blow on the point of the jaw, and banged his head against the wall.

Bill's luck was in ; the rifle-butt, only an inch from the floor, dropped with an infinitesimal sound. Furthermore, the muzzle, caught in the guard's clothing, held the rifle upright long enough for Bill to smash home another punishing blow.

The Mohmand was out from the first punch, and he swayed from the knees. Bill caught him, lowered him gently, and made a grab for the rifle.

Holding his breath, Bill listened. A man muttered in his sleep several yards away, but there came no other sign that the disturbance had been noted. The snoring went on unchecked, and Bill allowed himself a deep breath.

He would have liked to have gagged and bound the Mohmand, but first he must discover whether the inner cave was occupied by the Mullah or Orlof. Bill was banking on there being other caves behind, for he had seen no sign of sleeping kit in the cave.

With the stealth of a hunting cat he slid past the thick curtains and into the Mullah's "office." No sound could be heard there, the curtains effectually cutting off any noise from the outer cavern.

Returning to where he had left the Mohmand, Bill braced himself for the task of lifting the man. He could not afford to leave him lying where he was. The effect of a knock-out blow may last half a minute, five minutes, but seldom longer, and Bill needed more time than that to get a wireless message through to Peshawar.

With sweat springing out on his face Bill managed to carry the inert guard into the inner cave. Lowering him gently he took off the man's turban, grateful for the custom by which this form of headgear consisted of several yards of cloth. Bill's knife halved the turban ; he swiftly gagged the man, and then tied his wrists and ankles together.

"That'll hold you, my lad," Bill muttered, and stood upright to make sure of his bearings. A mental picture of the inner cave showed him the wireless over to the right, in the corner near the curtained opening through which John Staines had been brought for his mock execution.

Carefully feeling his way across the cave, Bill

reached the wireless set. The cabinet was closed and locked. Bill unsheathed his strong knife and inserted the blade under the lid near the lock.

Bracing himself for a slow turn, so that the least possible noise would be made when he forced the lock, Bill began to lever. Then he stopped, a thrill running through him. He had heard a sudden quick intake of breath. There was some one else in the room.

The sound came from less than a yard away. Withdrawing his knife, Bill reversed it, clasping the hilt so that he could use the haft as a club.

The silence was nerve-racking. The breathing was no longer audible, yet Bill knew he was not alone. Whoever was in the cave had not moved, but was waiting for some sign from Bill. A duel of courage and nerve followed—a desperate wait for some move, some little sign which would betray the exact position of the other.

Bill won. He heard the faint slurring sound of a foot moving across the thick carpet. The noise was the faintest possible, and in any but that brooding quiet would have passed unnoticed. Bill jumped, his left hand going out at what he considered would be throat height, his right hand, clasping the clubbed knife, striking viciously.

Both hands missed their objective, for the other man was crouching, and Bill gasped as a bony fist took him shrewdly in the stomach. A moment later his assailant rose from his stooping position, and the crown of his head caught Bill a terrific blow under the chin, causing a multitude of stars to flash before his eyes. He tried to strike with his clubbed knife even as his knees sagged, but the other man had already grabbed his wrist. An expert twist, which brought a groan of pain from Bill's lips, deprived him of his weapon. Then he was floored by a ju-jitsu hold.

" Make the least sound, you swine," a voice hissed in Pushtu, " and I'll break your arm like a rotten stick."

Bill gasped, and despite his pain managed a grim chuckle.

" Pax, Staines. I'm Bill Night of the S.S."

A gasp of amazement followed this announcement. The grip on Bill's arm slackened the least bit.

" Bill Night, are you ? What's your number in the Secret Service ? "

Bill gave the required information, and other details which only he could supply. Staines was convinced, and heaved a sigh of relief as he loosed his hold.

" By gosh, John, I must learn that hold you put

on me," murmured Bill as he gently massaged his upper arm and shoulder. "I thought I was a gone coon until you spoke. How long have you been free? I was coming to try and get a wireless message through to Peshawar."

"Same here. I've been free for about an hour, but I've lain doggo until I was sure the Mullah and his partners were fast asleep."

"Partners?" Bill queried, as he took the knife Staines had held out, and once more inserted the blade beneath the lid of the wireless cabinet. "I only know one, the gentleman named Orlof who seems to delight in impersonating you."

"There's another, who only came to-day."

Staines was about to tell Bill about the Semite when the curtains dividing the inner and outer caverns were pushed aside, and a hoarse voice whispered in Pushtu:

"Are you there, Hasrat Ali? We're changing the guard."

Bill and John Staines "froze." Bill Night had overlooked this possibility of the guard being changed while he was in the inner cavern.

A moment of silence followed; then the voice spoke again, this time more urgently.

" Hasrat Ali—where are you ? "

There was no answer. The curtains swung down with a soft rustle. The two Britishers heaved a sigh of relief ; but their relief was short lived, for at once beneath the curtains appeared the pale yellow glow of a lamp on the other side. The Mohmand in charge of the guard was bringing a light to see if the missing sentry was himself looting in the Mullah's inner cave.

CHAPTER NINE

" BANG goes our chance of sending a radio warning to Peshawar," Bill growled as he made for the heavy curtains. " Even if we could hide in here, this chap will raise the roof when he finds his man tied up."

" We've got to try and silence him," said John Staines grimly, " and take a chance of getting out if we fail. Are you alone ? "

" Got Clay Armstrong in the outer cave," Bill replied, and crouched as footsteps sounded on the other side of the curtain.

A moment later the Mohmand in charge of the guard swept the curtains aside, and held his lamp up to look into the Mullah's sanctum. For a moment he did not see the huddled form on the floor to his left. Bill seized his chance, and once more those iron hard knuckles rasped heavily against a Mohmand's chin.

The blow, unluckily, was not a knock-out, for the man had caught a momentary glimpse of the Britisher, and had instinctively moved. Bill's blow was more in the nature of a gliding punch, and while it staggered the man it did not put him down.

The lamp dropped out of his hands, the glass shattered, and the light flared up as oil splashed out of the container. Bill struck again, but the Mohmand was already yelling an alarm. The second blow took the man in the solar plexus, and he doubled up, gasping for breath.

From the outer cave came cries of alarm; the guards at the cave mouth shouted, and everywhere in the gloom the Mohmands stirred and started up, feeling for rifles.

"Come on," Bill grunted. "We've got to get out, quick."

A commanding yell from some side entry gave warning that one of the leaders was coming to investigate. Several lamps threw a yellow glow into the confusion at the mouth of the cave; men were milling about and asking what had happened. Many of them began surging towards the open, and behind this main body Bill and Staines went forward, only to be brought to an abrupt halt a matter of five yards from the entrance. The guards, realizing that whatever was wrong had happened inside the cave, were preventing their brethren from leaving.

"Stand fast—stand fast!" they shouted. "Something is afoot in the Mullah's cave! Be calm and make a search!"

" Where's your assistant ? " muttered John Staines. " We can't leave without him ! "

As if in direct answer to this query Clay Armstrong appeared at Bill's side. He had a rifle in one hand, two " plum " bombs in the other.

" Which will you have, sir ? " he asked.

Bill took the rifle, quietly reversed it, and nodded to Clay.

" Chuck your bombs among this little lot," he said. " As soon as they explode, yell out, and make a rush for the outside."

Save for a grumbling among the tribesmen there was now quietness in the cave. The Mullah, Orlof, and the Semite had appeared at the far end, and by the light of a lamp were examining the winded Mohmand. Between his gasps the man was trying to explain what had happened.

Clay Armstrong tossed his bombs in the air, aiming to drop them right in the middle of the huddled tribesmen. In the three seconds which followed, a couple of Mohmands began to speak ; they had been struck by the falling " plums."

Then the bombs exploded with two vivid yellowish-pink flashes at ground level. Bedlam broke loose, with screams of pain from men whose bare legs were scorched, and yells of surprise and alarm from the rest. The crowd in the cave tried to scatter; Bill led his companions into the confusion; men staggered away, cursing, as his rifle-butt found their turbaned heads. Clay Armstrong and John Staines followed, punching hard at all who came in their way, until the three of them reached the guards who stood at the cave entrance.

" Gas ! " screeched Bill. " Gas ! Get into the open or ye die ! "

The guards hesitated, raising their rifles to halt the three men, but Bill swung his weapon by the barrel, and one man went down without a murmur as the butt crashed on his turbaned pate. Another screamed as the return swing took him in the ribs. Then the Britishers were in the clean, cold night air.

" Down the hill ! " yelled Bill, this time in English, to give no clue to the Mohmands. The latter, recovering from their surprise, were already following at a run. The steeply sloping ground was littered with boulders and rough stones of all sizes; a man who fell there risked at least a broken leg.

Crack, crack, crack ! Rifles spat viciously from the mouth of the cave ; the guards had only one argument left for the men who had assaulted them. Bullets hummed past the fugitives, to flatten against the stones. A screech of anger followed the bullets ; the Mullah had discovered that his prisoner was missing.

"Follow them ! Five thousand rupees to the men who bring them back, dead or alive ! "

"We're worth something now," panted Clay Armstrong, as he slid past a boulder with the loss of an inch of skin from one of his knees. "Whew, that was a near one ! " A bullet had droned past his head with a sound like a homing bee.

From behind came the clatter of stones dislodged by the feet of Mohmands anxious to earn five thousand rupees. Bill Night turned beside a boulder and emptied the magazine of his rifle, checking the mad pursuit, but bringing a whistling hail of lead in reply. He escaped, being sheltered by the boulder, but John Staines was not so lucky, for a bullet took him in the right arm.

The Political Agent was now some thirty yards farther downhill ; Clay Armstrong was helping him along, for imprisonment had left him shaky about the legs. On level ground he would have been all right, but a man needed the spongy pads of a camel, the agility of a gazelle, and the surefootedness of a goat to travel at speed down such a hillside.

When the bullet struck him Staines swung round, breaking loose Clay's clutch on his arm, and crashed heavily to the ground. Clay, bending over him, found him stunned and inert.

There was a lull in the firing ; the Mohmands were waiting for Bill Night to fire again and give them an indication of his whereabouts. But Bill had already started downhill, having first thrown a chunk of rock as hard as he could away to the right. The sound of the falling rock, and the cascade of smaller stuff which went with it drew the Mohmands' fire again, and drowned the rattle of Bill's progress.

" *Bill ! Bill !* "

The urgent cry, just audible through the rattle of rifles, drew Bill across to where Clay was easing John Staines into a more comfortable position.

" I think he's been hit." Clay hastened to explain as Bill knelt down beside the unconscious man.

" And the last taxi gone home," said Bill, who could tell that Clay was beginning to feel the strain. " There isn't even an Ericsson Police Pillar in sight where we could ring up an ambulance."

" I'll run home and fetch my balloon, if you like," snorted Clay.

Bill smiled, for Clay was evidently feeling better.

" D'you know where he was hit ? " he asked, feeling John Staines for a tell-tale dampness.

" I'd say it was on his right side. He swung round from there as if something had kicked him."

Running his hand gently along the coat sleeve, Bill discovered the wound. Meanwhile, every minute or two, the Mohmands made the night hideous with a volley fired down the far side of the slope. Bill's stratagem in throwing the rock had misled them for the time being.

Bill tore a piece off the shirt of his Rajput uniform and gently bound up the injured arm. As soon as this was done he lifted the Political Agent across his broad shoulders.

" Come behind me, Clay, old man," he said, " and be ready to make a grab if I slip."

Very slowly they moved downhill, taking care to make a minimum of noise. The sounds of firing grew more and more infrequent, and finally died away. The Mohmands might be returning to the cave, or spreading in a cordon in the hope of encircling the fugitives.

After about ten minutes John Staines began to groan, and Bill laid him down. When the Political Agent came to his senses his first request was for a drink, but there was no water available.

"Sorry, John," said Bill, "but we'll have to wait until daylight comes, and then chance coming across a stream."

"Let's . . . be . . . moving," Staines muttered, and tried weakly to get to his feet. Bill and Clay took turns in supporting him ; when the first pale light of dawn was beginning to touch the hilltops they discovered a little nullah which—unlike most nullahs—was clothed in lush vegetation, a sign that a spring supplied the earth with moisture throughout the year.

Clay spent fifteen minutes trying to find the spring and finally located a stretch of what appeared to be sphagnum moss. Never had water tasted so sweet as that which oozed upwards when he pressed his face into the moss.

With nothing to carry water in, their only course was to get John Staines across to the spring. Once there, he drank feverishly. His face was flushed, his eyes were bright, and it was plain that his wound and the fall had broken what remained of a strength already sapped by imprisonment. John Staines was a hospital case.

Bill took off the bloodstained bandage. The bullet had gone through the muscle of the upper arm, fortunately missing bone and artery. Bill washed and bandaged the wound while John Staines lay in an uneasy sleep.

" We're in a mess now," Clay ventured at length. " We ought to be getting word to one of the Pass forts, or there'll be war before we can say ' chips.' What about it, sir ? Will you go, while I stay with him ? It seems pretty hopeless for us to . . ."

John Staines interrupted. He had opened his eyes as Clay spoke, and there was desperate purpose in them.

" Listen, Bill," he muttered. " You've got to leave me and get word to Peshawar. Yesterday afternoon I heard the Mullah and Orlof talking with a Semite named Yakub. This is no political trouble ; they're organizing a raid on Peshawar, to loot the city and cantonment."

He moistened his lips, and Bill made him drink again from the ice-cold water oozing out of the moss.

" Gosh, that's better," said Staines, and now his voice was stronger. "There's a 'plane, marked with the British rings . . . it's going to bomb as many villages as possible, to rouse the tribes. There's a punitive column coming into the Khyber to-day to punish the men who robbed the caravan. The tribes-men will attack Landi Kotal, Ali Masjid, and Jamrud.

Result, there'll be a hurried call for help from Peshawar
. . . and to-night the Mullah's chosen men will march
into Peshawar in Rajput uniforms . . . while others in
tribesmen's rig-out make a mock attack on the
cantonment."

Staines passed a hand wearily over his brow, and
went on.

"This Semite, Yakub, has agents in both city and
cantonment . . . everything is ready for the disguised
Mohmands to march to the bank and loot it, and
then loot the city bazaar. You know what wealth
there is in the Street of the Silversmiths. They'll get
away with it; the soldiers and police left in the
cantonment will be repelling the mock attack."

Clay was staring down at the injured Political
Agent.

"Lumme, sir," he said, "it seems a lot of fuss for
this Mullah to make just to stage a robbery."

Staines shook his head.

"No, it isn't. By stirring up the tribesmen he
takes the bulk of the soldiers out of the barracks. No
one expects a raid when there's fighting in the Khyber.
It has never happened before. The Mullah has spotted
the one weakness in the scheme of defence. He
estimates they'd get a quarter of a million pounds in

bullion and jewels. I fancy they'd get more than that . . . and they've got to be stopped."

"They have," agreed Clay, and turned to Bill for orders.

Bill knelt on the ground, pondering. Daylight was spreading on the frontier ; a humming noise gave warning of a distant 'plane, either an army 'plane reconnoitring for the force starting out from Peshawar, or the machine used by the Mullah to stir the tribes to action. Presently the listening Britishers had an answer to their unspoken questions ; the muffled *whump* of a bomb explosion shook the clear morning air.

"I'm going," said Bill. "I'll leave Clay to look after you, John, and get help here as soon as possible."

The Political Agent opened his eyes wearily ; as Bill's words sank home he sat up, gritting his teeth with the effort.

"As Political Agent for the Border," he said, a steely note in his voice, "I order you both to go and to leave me here. The tribes will be picketing all the hills between here and the Khyber . . . and one man may die. We can't afford to take a chance. There's too much at stake. Quite apart from the loot, if the Mullah gets away with this raid there'll be others to follow it, Border war after Border war, and a lot of bloodshed before things are settled."

"We can't leave you like this," protested Bill. "I'll get through all right. Clay can scour around until he finds a goatherd who'll supply you with milk, and . . ."

"Bill, as a man I appreciate your thought for me," John Staines said firmly. "God knows I don't want to die any more than the next man. I've got a wife and a bonny little two-year-old boy." His voice wavered a little, then with an effort he stiffened himself. "We've not to think about those things, Bill. We're here to do a job . . . and that job is to keep the peace on the Border. That peace can best be assured if you two leave me, and get word to Peshawar as fast as you can."

Bill's face was stern; a muscle twitched in his left cheek. It might be easy to talk of duty when a man sat in his club, with his feet up and cool drinks by his side; it was hard to leave a brave man lying wounded in the blazing heat with the fever-light in his eyes.

A line from some long-forgotten poem came into his mind : " *Only the game fish swim upstream.*"

John Staines was " swimming upstream " now,

trying to make doubly sure the failure of the Mullah's raid on Peshawar.

"If ever any one deserved the V.C., you do, John," said Bill Night grimly. "I'm obeying your order; you *are* my superior officer. I salute you as that, and as a *man*. *Au revoir* . . . because I'm coming back for you."

"*Au revoir*."

John Staines managed a smile.

"If folks at home knew half the things men like him do," said Clay with a break in his voice, "there'd be better pay than there is, and more blinking medals at the end of it. If he comes through he'll get a couple of lines in a newspaper . . . to fill up a corner in the women's fashion page, or something like that."

"That'll be enough of that," said Bill gently. "Clay, we've a man's job to do, and talking slush won't help John Staines or the other people who are working for permanent peace in the Khyber."

"Sorry, sir. You're right. We get paid for these jobs . . . and what the newspapers say afterwards shouldn't worry us."

They looked back before they topped a ridge, and waved cheerily to the recumbent figure behind them; then they set their faces towards the Khyber.

Meanwhile, every minute or two brought the muffled sound of a bomb explosion. The Mullah's airman, in a 'plane made to look like a British machine, was bombing the villages systematically. By the time he had finished his deadly work the tribesmen would need little encouragement from the Mullah to attack the Khyber forts. " A life for a life " is the hillman's law ; if the British bombed him, he would retaliate by trying to wipe out the Feringhis who stewed in the terrific heat at Jamrud, Ali Masjid, and Landi Kotal.

Even as the two Secret Service men were making their way cautiously through deep valleys and rocky nullahs, the tribesmen were hurrying their women and children to caves, and preparing to launch fierce attacks on the forts. Word had already gone forth that two men dressed as Rajput soldiers, and a white man in ordinary clothing would try to reach Ali Masjid. They were to be shot down like dogs. The hills near the Pass were picketed by hawk-eyed tribesmen, watching for the trio who had escaped from the Mullah's clutches. The fugitives, if seen, would be greeted by a withering blast of bullets.

Ali Masjid Gorge. Such was the barrage of bullets that the car was put out of action; after one more attempt the military decided not to try again. Instead they sent a couple of bombing 'planes over to Landi Kotal to harass the tribesmen who were attacking that fort.

Orlof slapped Yakub on the back when the last message was received.

"Most of the troops stationed at Peshawar must have come out to the Pass," he chuckled. "We shall have little difficulty to-night."

"Thanks to me," Yakub said sourly. "For I have done all the dangerous work. I organized the men who will be waiting to enter the Bankers' Bazaar. I made the arrangements for watchmen, keys, and guards."

Orlof gave him a sidelong look.

"And who provided the necessary money?" he asked tartly. "Who paid for the aeroplane, who found Sikh uniforms for the raid on the caravan, who paid for the uniforms we are wearing now? The Mullah and myself! Don't forget that each of us has contributed an equal share, whether in cash or courage."

Another shrug of the shoulders from the Semite, and they went on their way.

One last wireless message was received while the raiders were in hiding a mile or so from Peshawar city, waiting for darkness to fall.

" Runners have just come back to say that two of the three men who escaped last night have been seen trying to get through to the Pass, but were driven back. They may try to reach Peshawar. Better watch for them."

Orlof looked at the Semite.

" What do you think we ought to do ? It's impossible for us to guard all the little trails from here which lead to the city."

The Semite screwed up his eyes. He thought for a moment, then smiled.

" They will be dog-tired," he said, " and are certain to try to enter the city by the Bajauri Gate. They will, if I reason correctly, try to telephone from the guard-house there to the authorities in the cantonment. By so doing they will save forty minutes' walking. We can take care of them."

" I hope you aren't making a mistake," said Orlof coldly.

" I never make mistakes," Yakub declared. " I know these trails too well to make mistakes. They will go to the Bajauri Gate."

Twenty minutes later darkness came like the drawing of a curtain over the western sky. The disguised Mohmands were drawn up in ranks of three, their rifles at the slope ; with Orlof and Yakub at their head, they marched down on to the main road which led to Peshawar city, and the east gate which was called Bajauri.

The rest of the raiders were divided into two parties. One would strike at the south side of the cantonment, the other at the north side of the city. With the bulk of the soldiers in the Khyber Pass, all available men would be rushed to the threatened positions ; and according to the scheme worked out by the wily Yajub, the Bajauri Gate would have only a small guard, and there would be few, if any, soldiers in the centre of the city.

In the cantonment Yakub's men, chosen thieves, would enter the principal bank. Their preparations had been completed weeks before. The loot would be hidden in the cantonment, and removed at leisure when the hullabaloo consequent on the raid had died down.

The Bajauri Gate had been closed for the night when the steady tramp of feet brought a challenge from the sentry. Orlof, prompted by Yakub, who had studied very carefully the routine which took place when troops wished to enter Peshawar after darkness, gave the correct answers. The heavy gate bars were taken down, the brass studded doors swung open, and at a curt word of command from Orlof the raiders marched in.

The British soldiers guarding the gate, sixteen all told, were standing idly about, watching. The two sentries, the only armed men, were presenting arms as the supposed Rajput soldiers marched in.

" Things must have quietened down a bit in the Pass," the sergeant was thinking, when with appalling ferocity the disguised Mohmands attacked the guard. No weapons were used. The Semite had very wisely decreed that no one should be hurt, for a wounded man may scream out with pain and raise the alarm. A man who is knocked on the head hasn't time to scream.

In a couple of minutes the raiders were in command of the gate, and the men on guard were being taken into the guardroom, where they were speedily tied up and gagged.

Yakub left ten men to watch the gate.

" In ten minutes time," he said, " firing will break out to the north. You, Ali, must be ready to answer the telephone. Assure the man who rings up that all is quiet at this gate; then no more soldiers will be rushed here. Is that understood?"

It was understood. Orlof and Yakub formed up their ninety men and marched them into the city. Of spectators there had been none, for when the city gates are closed there is no reason for any of the inhabitants of Peshawar to stay in the vicinity. The beggars had been moved on, and the hawkers had gone when the sun went down.

Ten minutes later, as the raiders were marching rhythmically towards the Bankers' Bazaar, a sudden burst of firing broke out. Orlof halted his men. The people who thronged the streets looked uneasily at one another. The firing was resumed after a momentary pause. Then it ceased, and in the dead silence which seemed to have fallen over the city there sounded the thin wailing note of a bugle sounding the alarm.

Before the bugle call was finished firing broke out again, and then, as the populace began to hurry to their homes, hoping to get indoors before any raiders entered the city, the lights failed. Yakub's men were working with clocklike precision; the party detailed to cut off the electricity supply in the cantonment had done their work well.

Yakub produced a torch. Orlof did likewise.

Yakub gathered about him half the men, and proceeded in the direction of the Bankers' Bazaar; Orlof took the other half and went off towards the Street of the Silversmiths. The Semite had made elaborate plans for robbing three banks in the Bazaar. Elaborate plans were not necessary in the Street of the Silversmiths. Strong men could break down doors, and the threat of a cut throat would soon induce a Kashmiri or Hindu silversmith to open his cases of treasure.

Meanwhile Verey lights were going into the air from the perimeter wall about the cantonments, and from behind the barbed wire the hastily assembled troops were firing steadily at the rifle flashes which marked the position of the raiding Mohmands.

At the Bajauri Gate the telephone bell rang harshly. An anxious officer who had gathered his small force about him asked:

"What are conditions at Bajauri?"

A Mohmand who could speak English well gave the reassuring answer.

"All quiet here, sir. Not a shot has been fired."

"Good! Stay on the alert, and if you are attacked ring me up at once, though I doubt if I'll be able to spare any men. There's a determined attack being made on the North Gate."

" Very good, sir."

The Mohmand hung up the receiver with a smile. There would be no interference with the Bajauri Gate, and in less than an hour the Semite and Orlof would be returning with much loot. The whole of the raiders would be able to slip out of the city as easily and quietly as they had entered, to return to the hills and deliver to the Mullah such spoil as could at once be removed.

At that moment Bill Night and Clay Armstrong reached the Bajauri Gate. They had spent the day sneaking through the hills, after four vain attempts to reach the fort in Ali Masjid Gorge. The watchers on the hills had been almost too much for them. Both men were dog tired. They had eaten nothing since the previous night, and scrambling along sun-baked, rock-strewn hills and nullahs was work for well-fed men. For the last two miles Bill had been helping Clay along.

Banging on the gate, Bill called out in a husky voice :

" Open up . . . I have an important message from the Khyber." He spoke in English, for he was pretty certain that an English guard would be on the gate, especially as the sham attack being staged to the north was now in full swing.

Clay had sunk down on his heels, his back to the crumbling stonework of the wall. He was exhausted, and would have given almost anything for a quart of icy water. Springs in the Khyber hills are few and far between.

Bill hammered on the gate again, calling out to the guard. Then the wicket opened, a light was shone on the Secret Service man's face, temporarily blinding him. Then a hoarse voice called out in Pushtu :

" Ali . . . Ali. Open the gate."

Bill started, a frown creasing his face. He had expected to find white soldiers guarding the gate ! Suspicion darkened his tired mind. Neither Rajput nor Sikh nor Ghurka spoke the Pushtu. He turned, a warning shout on his lips, but at that moment the gate was opened, and half a dozen Mohmands hurled themselves on him.

The struggle was brief, but bitter. Bill fought like a lion. He found new strength from somewhere, and his fist cracked home on several jaws before he was finally subdued and carried through the gate into the city.

Clay Armstrong, dozing when the attack was made, came to life, half rose, and then relaxed. Quick to count the odds, he realized that this was an occasion for discretion rather than valour.

When the gates were banged shut, and the bolts once more slammed into place, Clay rose. The night still echoed with the rattle of rifle fire and the staccato hammering of a machine-gun.

" No use going up there," he muttered. " Both sides would probably pot at me. I've got to do something on my own, quickly."

Forgetting his weary muscles, he leaned against the wall, closed his eyes, and thought hard. After a minute he got up, turned north, and walked as quickly as he could along the foot of the wall. He had remembered that this wall was crumbling in places. At several points the weather-worn stonework made it possible for an active man to get over. Barbed wire guarded these points, but a determined man who was prepared to lose a little skin might get through.

Limping along, Clay finally came to a weak spot. The ground was littered with fallen stonework ; feeling for hand-holds, the weary Britisher began his attempt. Twice he was forced back, the hand-holds petering out. The third time he was successful. He edged this way and that, gaining a foot at this place, two feet at that, zigzagging up the wall until finally his hand encountered barbed wire.

Clinging by each hand in turn, Clay managed

somehow to take off his soiled and torn Rajput tunic, and to put it on back to front so that the sleeves would protect his hands. Then he essayed the task of creeping through the barbed wire.

Many an exclamation of pain was wrung from him before he finally stood on the city wall, breathing in the cool night air which was sweeping eastward to the Punjab from beyond the darkly dangerous Khyber.

Peshawar city lay at his feet, black as a pool of ink, save that here and there he could see tiny yellow glimmers, where some one who had an oil lamp could laugh at the fact that the electricity supply had unaccountably failed.

At intervals along the wall were stone steps leading down to the narrow alleyways of the city. In the days before the might of Britain brought Peshawar some immunity from raiding Pathans, those stone steps had been used by men who tumbled out of their string charpoy beds to repel raiders. Clay found the nearest flight and felt his way cautiously down to street level. Next, he must either go for help or see what he could do at the Bajauri Gate. He thought for a moment of making his way to the threatened North Gate, but realized that time was on the Mullah's side. To reach the North Gate he would have to wander for perhaps

Then he essayed the task of creeping through the barbed wire.

half an hour among alleys dark as the Styx ; then he would have to convince the officer in charge that he was British, and that something more serious was taking place than long-range firing from beyond the city walls.

Kicking out at a pi-dog which got between his feet, Clay lurched away towards the Bajauri Gate. His teeth were clenched, and by the time he reached the guardhouse he was reeling with fatigue.

Pulling himself together, he crept forward with the stealth of a hunting cat. No near voice or other sound broke the quiet of this corner of the old city. The crackle of rifles from the north was like the off-stage noises in a play.

The Mohmands guarding the raiders' way of escape were all picked men. They were crouching at vantage points from which, if necessary, they could sweep the approach to the gate with rifle fire. No trouble was anticipated from the guardroom, where a solitary Mohmand waited inside the doorway, immobile as the Sphinx.

Clay listened for several minutes, straining his ears. Finally he decided that the gate had been deserted, and the men who had captured Bill Night had gone looting.

Drawing a deep breath, he tiptoed round the side

of the guardhouse, scurried into the doorway, and collided with the squatting Mohmand tribesman. The latter, a six-foot warrior, clasped a modern Lee-Enfield rifle, which clattered to the floor as the gasping Clay bowled its owner over into the darkness of the building. A voice called from across the road, asking if anything was wrong.

While the Mohmand was struggling to his feet Clay turned and slammed the door shut. He felt for the key, found it in the lock, and with a mighty wrench turned it. No one could come in for a little while ; but the cursing Mohmand grunted with relief as he found his fallen rifle.

With his back to the door Clay stood for a second waiting, unarmed. Then he threw himself down face foremost.

Crack ! The rifle spat flame above him, fired from the hip, and aimed so as to hit even a crouching man.

CHAPTER ELEVEN

THE officer who had recommended Clay Armstrong for the Secret Service some two and a half years previously had made no mistake. He had said that Clay possessed a cool brain, quick wits, and amazing courage ; and now Clay displayed all three of these gifts at once. The bullet buried itself in the stout woodwork of the door ; by the red flash the Mohmand saw him, but Clay grabbed his opponent's ankle, and with a mighty heave unbalanced him.

A downward jab with the rifle barrel missed the Britisher by inches. Clay staggered up, jerking the muscular ankle he held, and the Mohmand went over backwards ; his roaring oaths were cut off as his head thudded on the cement floor.

Meanwhile others of the gate guard had come hurrying across, and now were gathered at the door, demanding to know what was happening. Clay leaped on the fallen Mohmand, and despite the fact that the man was limp, grabbed his beard and banged his head twice again.

" That'll keep you quiet a bit longer," he grunted, and felt for the man's rifle.

As he picked it up a butt smashed the panes and wooden frame of the window. A figure appeared in the window-space, limned against the black of the sky. The disguised Mohmands wanted no more shooting ; one of their number was entering to investigate, a knife between his teeth. Clay, admiring his bravery, dropped on one knee and shot him.

The Mohmand crumpled up and fell heavily forward into the room. Clay, breathing hard now, dodged away from his position. It was as well that he did so, for the other Mohmands abandoned their attempt at silence and poured a volley of shots through the window.

The lead splashed into shapeless streaks along the stone walls. Clay had darted forward, so that he was beneath the broken window. He poked the barrel of his rifle over the ledge, and fired again without aiming.

Luck was with him. A scream rang out, followed by the sound of hurried footsteps. The Mohmands did not care for this form of fighting. Hand to hand work in the dark with knives they could face, although they preferred distant shooting in the hills. Clay fired again, and was answered by another volley. Bullets ricochetted round the room. In the grim silence which followed, Clay wondered how many cartridges were left in the magazine of his rifle, and whether he could find the stunned Mohmand's stock of ammunition. Then he heard a sound from near by.

Thump-bump-bump-bump !

A cold thrill ran down Clay's spine ; for a moment he thought the Mohmand must have recovered his senses. Then the sound was repeated, with something rhythmic about it.

" Bump, bump, bump . . . scrape, scrape, scrape . . . bump, bump, bump. Bump, bump, bump . . . scrape, scrape, scrape . . . bump, bump, bump."

"*Morse !* " murmured Clay. " Morse code . . . S O S . . . I'll bet that's Bill ! "

Clay was wrong. It was the sergeant of the imprisoned guard trying to attract his attention.

Clay fired another shot through the window, and crawled across the floor until one hand encountered a pair of heavily nailed ammunition boots. A touch on the puttee-wrapped legs, and Clay breathed more easily. He slithered across to the limp Mohmand, took his knife, and was shortly engaged in cutting free the first of the British soldiers who had been so neatly overwhelmed, and then bound and gagged, by the bogus Rajputs.

The rest of the soldiers were rapidly freed, and the sergeant hurried into the rear room. From a cupboard he took a heavy pistol and charged it with a Verey light.

"I'll show them blanketty-blank hoodlums where they get off," he growled. "Sneaking up on us dressed in the King's uniform."

He leaned out of the broken window, fired his Verey pistol in the air, and ducked down as he pulled the trigger ; that action saved his life, for at once half a dozen bullets smashed into the room.

"Open that window at the back, lads," the sergeant ordered, "and five of you get through. Fix bayonets, and when you're ready we'll give 'em a plastering from this side, just to take their minds off other things. Get the idea, Marmadook ? "

The man addressed as "Marmadook" grunted assent. Six of the soldiers squirmed out of the guard-house by way of a window in the back room. They fixed their bayonets, and crept round to the side of the building. Meanwhile the others had taken their rifles from the rack where they had been chained ; having loaded, they waited in the darkness.

" I'm goin' to fire a couple of shots," the sergeant whispered. "They'll reply. When you get an idea where the roosters are, pepper 'em to glory an' back."

The men huddled on either side of the window of the room, where they were safe from anything but a ricochetting bullet. The sergeant poked his rifle over the window-ledge and fired twice.

A Mohmand bullet struck a spark from his rifle barrel as he fired the second shot, but a moment later the Britishers opened a withering fire which brought several tribesmen down. As it ceased the group with bayonets fixed charged from cover yelling like madmen.

This was more than the Mohmands could stand. They broke and fled, melting like shadows into the dark alleys.

Clay had dragged Bill Night into the back room, and by dint of vigorously slapping his face and pinching his ears had brought him round. Bill was still a little dazed, but a little more of this rough treatment effectively cleared his head.

Meanwhile the sergeant of the guard was trying to telephone to the officer commanding the defence forces. The firing at the North Gate was still going on unabated, although no attempt had been made to force an entry. The raiders remained in position, despite the dropping of several high explosive bombs from a 'plane hurriedly sent up from the nearby flying ground.

"Can't get no reply from the C.O.," the sergeant grumbled. Then he remembered that he did not know who his mysterious visitors were, and asked them to identify themselves.

"I know you're not blinkin' Pathans," he said apologetically, "but all the same I'm supposed to keep a strict tally on any one coming in through the gate at night."

Before Bill could begin to explain, one of the soldiers came in.

"Some cars coming, sergeant," he said. "At least they've stopped about a hundred yards away, and they doused their lights at once."

Bill Night, whose head was now aching, but quite clear, grasped the situation; in a few words he told the sergeant how the raid had taken place.

"Those cars will be loaded with loot," he said. "We've got to stop them from leaving the city."

"Well, we'll shed a little light on the subject," the sergeant growled. "'Opkins, bring me some more o' them Verey lights. The rest of you take what cover you can outside, and be ready to give the blighters some rapid fire . . . if I says so."

The soldiers went outside, lay down, and waited. The sergeant fired his pistol. The Verey light sailed up and exploded ; from the little parachute which began to descend a brilliant magnesium flare lit up the whole scene.

A number of men in Rajput uniform were hastily unloading three lorries ; their swarming activity was for all the world like that of a disturbed nest of ants.

" Shift them, sergeant," snapped Bill. " We must keep those lorry-loads intact."

" Fire ! " commanded the sergeant coolly, as though he were ordering a platoon of training recruits on a rifle range.

The crash of the volley was followed by cries of pain and anger from the lorries. There was a momentary scattering ; then the raiders flung themselves down and began to return the fire. Although it is very hard to shoot a man lying prone on the ground, the Mohmands were born marksmen, and bullets began to whistle close. One man gasped as a bullet nicked his shoulder. Another's cap was whisked off his head. The sergeant fired another Verey light, and with this assistance the soldiers managed to drop several of those still frantically unloading the first lorry.

For ten minutes this fight went on. Then the Mohmands ceased firing, and by rolling over and over they reached the edges of the roadway, where they were able to gain their feet and vanish down narrow side streets. At length, when several Verey lights had failed to show any signs of life about the lorries, the sergeant turned to Bill with a triumphant smile.

" Reckon that's driven 'em off, sir," he said. " Them fellers can't stand the fire of disciplined troops. It's always the same. In a flurry they're all right. Ambush work is what they specializes in."

Bill was scarcely listening ; he believed that the Mohmands would not have sneaked off so quietly unless they had managed to take the major portion of the loot with them.

After another few minutes of silence, and the firing of two more Verey lights, a patrol was sent out to investigate and found the deserted lorries practically empty. Bill looked grim ; so far the Mullah's raid had been a success. Unless the booty was recovered, the chance of lasting peace on the Khyber Border was gone. If the Feringhis could be tricked once, they could be tricked again, and many would be willing to try the same game.

"They'll maybe sneak out of the city the way I came in," suggested Clay Armstrong. "I came over the wall. Do you think . . ."

Bill turned to the sergeant.

"Get your men together," he snapped. "Clay's probably right. We may catch them yet."

Outside the city wall they went, leaving two men to guard the gate. Once more a Verey light rose ; the magnesium flare revealed dark shapes scrambling down ropes which hung from the top of the wall about three hundred yards north of the Bajauri Gate.

"Give 'em rapid fire, lads," the sergeant ordered, and again the rifles belched flame and lead. However, most of the bogus Rajput soldiers were already outside the city wall, and hurrying away into the darkness.

Some halted to reply to the fire directed against them, but a last few figures slithered down the ropes, and the whole body melted into the night. A few moments later a green Verey light was fired from about half a mile outside the wall—obviously a signal to the Mohmands who were still harassing the North Gate and the cantonment. Fire slackened almost immediately, and within five minutes city and cantonment were silent again. The raid had been brought to a successful conclusion.

An hour later Bill Night was closeted with a harassed C.O., who listened with bulging eyes to the Secret Service man's story. The lights had come on again ; police had managed to force their way into the electricity works, and had discovered the engineers bound and gagged. The Mullah's plans had been executed with admirable efficiency.

"How much loot they've got I don't know," Bill said gravely. "It was sufficient to load three lorries, and but for the soldiers on the Bajauri Gate they'd have got through there with ease. As it is we've got seven dead Mohmands and about fifteen wounded. Some loot is recovered, mainly from the Street of the Silversmiths ; it was all in sacks, about the weight a normal man could carry. They had everything ready."

"Well, if they get away with every ounce of silver and gold in both city and cantonment," the C.O. said grimly, "this Mullah fellow has to be brought in. A lot of the gilt will be taken off the hillman's gingerbread if his leader is captured. Night . . . do you think you can do anything ? It's no use our trying to follow these confounded raiders. They'll have scattered to the four winds, and be on every goat track for miles before sun-up."

Bill thought for a moment. He was tired and hungry and thirsty as any hunter. Yet he and Clay were the only men who could find the Mullah's cave.

"If you'll give us time for a meal, sir," he said cheerfully, "my assistant and I will do our level best."

"If you can bring in that Mullah," the C.O. said, "you'll have earned the heartfelt thanks of millions. What will you require?"

A scuffle of preparation followed. Bill gave his instructions and outlined his requirements. He and Clay took a shower-bath and ate a meal of gargantuan size.

An hour before dawn a big bomber took off and headed for the grim peaks which rise to the clouds on either side of the Khyber Pass.

CHAPTER TWELVE

FOR ten miles the bomber sped west, climbing all the time; then the pilot shut off his engine. Clay Armstrong looked at Bill. The silence was almost painful after the throbbing roar of the mighty Rolls-Royce motors.

" That's known as the 'silent approach,' " said Bill. " We can get over our objective without the sound of our engines giving notice that we are coming. We want to sneak in at the back door, so to speak; then we can give the Mullah a pleasant surprise."

Clay grinned, and held up his clenched fist as he spoke.

" ' One clout—laid out,' as they say in Lancashire. If I get half a chance that trouble-maker 'll be sorry for himself."

For a few minutes the only sound was a whistling of wind past the 'plane; then the pilot turned in his seat.

" We're about where you want to land," he said quietly. " I can see the winking light from Fort Ali Masjid."

Bill nodded and rose to his feet. By wireless message to Fort Ali Masjid the Commandant there had been asked to put a red light on his roof, so that the bomber pilot could tell when he was near the hill which contained the Mullah's cave. That winking red eye had come in for a lot of attention from snipers on the hills, but the soldier in charge of it was safe under cover.

" Count ten, after you've stepped out," the pilot warned them. " Then pull your release cord."

" Supposing I stammer ? " asked Clay, smiling. The pilot chuckled.

" Count two," he retorted, " and you'd better make it snappy."

Bill pushed open the door, no easy task with the wind trying to keep it closed. He stepped out, and was followed a few seconds later by Clay. The pilot banked, and headed back towards Peshawar, thinking as he flew how safe was the job of a bombing pilot compared with that of a Secret Service Agent.

" I wouldn't have leapt out over those hills for anything," he murmured. " Even if they make a safe landing they may get their throats cut two minutes afterwards."

Bill and Clay had jerked their parachute release

179

cords, and were wondering whether they would come down on a hill-top or glide gently into a valley.

They did neither, but landed rather uncomfortably on a stony hillside. The gentle wind which was blowing began to drag them, but a few shrewd slashes with their knives cut them free of their parachute harness ; the billowing 'chutes went rustling over the stones until they collapsed.

Dawn was coming swiftly. Cautiously flashing his light several times, Bill waited to see if Clay were anywhere near.

A hawk screamed shrilly, once, twice, three times. Bill cupped his hands about his mouth and sent a mournful goat's bleat into the chill morning air. Five minutes later the two men were together. The rapidly growing light enabled them to decide where they were. Without a word they began to scramble downhill. Some three miles away was the valley where they had left John Staines ; there was time to attend to him before they attempted to capture the Mullah.

Forty minutes later John Staines paused in the act of slaking his thirst again in the wet moss. Hearing the sound of approaching feet, he raised himself, and saw two bearded hillmen striding towards him. They appeared to be Mohmands, armed to the teeth.

"I thought it was too good to last," he muttered, and buried his face once more, drinking long and deep. Then he was hailed by a familiar voice; his head came up from the moss.

"Good-morning, John. How are you feeling?"

"Bill Night," Staines gasped. "I was thinking you two thugs meant the end of things. How'd you get here? Did you stop the raid?"

Bill shook his head. He sat down and produced from a pack some sandwiches and a thermos flask.

"Tuck in, John. Clay will attend to your arm. We can't stay long. We're due to handcuff the Mullah before his warriors return from Peshawar."

"Was the raid successful?" John asked anxiously. "I thought . . ."

"We couldn't get into the Pass," Bill interrupted. "Every peak was manned by snipers, so we had to give up the attempt, and make a detour through the hills to Peshawar."

He gave a brief summary of the events of the night, and spread before Staines the other contents of his pack.

"We're hoping to reach the Mullah's cave before his men get back. There's food here for about three days, an automatic, twenty rounds of ammunition, and a tribesman's dress. Rest, and when you feel fit enough to move, make your way across to Michni Fort. If things quieten down you may be able to reach Ali Masjid."

"I'd like to come with you," said John Staines, "but I'm afraid I'm too shaky."

"You get your strength back, John. You're more important to the Khyber as a live Political Agent than as a dead Secret Service man."

"Sounds as if you don't think much of your chances."

Bill laughed and quoted a saying of the hillmen.

"'A man can only die once.' If we can scotch the Mullah, what happens to us doesn't much matter."

"Good luck," said John Staines, holding out his hand. "I'll be thinking of you."

Bill and Clay shook hands with him, and turned up the valley again. In five minutes they were out of sight of the lonely wounded man. The pair now bore no resemblance to the men the Mullah had seen before. They both wore heavy beards and moustaches, and padding in Bill's cheeks made him appear heavy-featured ; a skilfully-moulded tin box packed behind his left shoulder-blade added deformity to his disguise.

Clay Armstrong seemed very broad in the body ;

around his waist was strapped a special 'bomber's apron,' in which he carried the means of sudden death for a number of men. At all costs the Mullah and his two chief followers had to be put out of action.

Both Bill and Clay were perspiring freely by the time they neared the Mullah's cave. They made no attempt to go cautiously. They approached from the Peshawar side, hoping to be taken for two of the raiders who had attacked Peshawar during the night.

Conscious, as they drew near the cave, that keen eyes were scrutinizing them, they climbed slowly upwards, as men climb who are weary. Bill and Clay were weary enough, for they had not slept for thirty-six hours; their eyes were sunken and red rimmed, and their condition plain to see.

When they were about fifty yards from the cave a gruff command in Pushtu halted them. From behind a rock a Mohmand stepped forth, rifle levelled from the hip.

" Who are ye, and what seek ye ? "

Bill looked up, and wiped a dirty hand across his bearded face before replying.

" We be two of those who went to Peshawar," he said. " We bring tidings from Orlof to the Mullah."

As a token of good faith they laid down their rifles

and dropped their heavy knives. At a curt word of command they advanced again, keyed up and ready for action. If any attempt was made to search them, Clay's bombs would at once be discovered.

Word had been sent into the cave to the Mullah, and a voice from the darkness bade the guard bring the two men in.

With a guard on either side of them, and one bringing up the rear, they once more entered the gloomy cave, where only a couple of small camel-dung fires were burning. The majority of the Mohmands were out with Orlof and the Semite. When they confronted the green-turbaned Mullah as he sat in the inner cave, Bill thought the leader's eyes had a strained look about them. Otherwise he was the same— swarthy, dark-eyed, with features cast in a European mould.

Bill and Clay bowed low.

" What news ? "

This time Clay spoke. The Mullah had never heard his voice, but might have recognized Bill's, even if it were disguised.

" The raid was successful, O Great One," Clay began. " All went as planned, save that we had some trouble at the Bajauri Gate. It was necessary to unload the three motor lorries and distribute the loot among the men. A few were left, killed or wounded—we had no time to make sure."

" Ye have done well," the Mullah said, his eyes gleaming with satisfaction. " How far in advance of the main body are ye ? "

" Not much, Great One," Clay said. " For though we were sent on in advance, we took a wrong path in the darkness."

" Ye have done well," the Mullah repeated.

Rising from his seat he came round the table and clapped Bill on the " deformed " shoulder. That token of goodwill was like dropping a match into a barrel of gunpowder ; the Mullah's hand hit the shaped tin box, which contained a number of things necessary to Bill's plan.

As if he had touched something red hot the Mullah leaped backwards.

" Hold them ! " he yelled, and his hand went beneath his cloak, apparently searching for a weapon.

Clay Armstrong whipped out a tiny automatic pistol. It had been up his baggy sleeve, and a shake brought it into his hand.

" One move from you, my friend," he said, " and I'll drop you dead in your tracks."

Bill Night had turned, neatly evading the out-stretched arms of the man behind him. He, too, now had a weapon in either hand. The Mohmands backed a pace or two, and then attacked fearlessly.

This was no time for squeamishness, and Bill shot the three men down. Not only his life and Clay's were at stake, but also the lives of hundreds of British soldiers and peaceful citizens of the Punjab. In a second the inner cave was wreathed with blue powder smoke, and filled with the curses of the Mullah and the groans of the injured men.

" Back to the far wall," Clay snarled, menacing the Mullah. "If you force me to shoot, I'll blow your brains out."

The Mullah was silent, and Clay realized that those curses had been spoken not in Pushtu, but in some language unknown to him, Clay Armstrong.

From the outer cave came the sound of running feet. A bearded Mohmand thrust aside the heavy curtains which acted as a door ; his eyes narrowed when he found himself staring at a couple of automatic pistols.

" Come in," Bill commanded, " or die where you stand."

The Mohmand came forward, eyes glittering evilly.

His nostrils twitched as he smelt powder smoke. Bill waved him to the side wall, and covering him with one weapon, waited for any other who might come.

Fifteen seconds later the curtains were pulled aside once more, and two more men stood in the entrance.

" Come in," Bill ordered, " and . . . ah, would you ? "

The curtain was dropped, but Bill's automatics spat flame and lead. The sound of falling bodies on the other side of the curtain testified to the deadly accuracy of his aim.

" Any more outside ? " snapped Bill, turning to the dazed Mohmand whom he had just trapped. The man shook his head, momentarily deprived of the power of speech.

" Back to that wall," Bill ordered, and the Mohmand ranged himself with the Mullah, within range of Clay's automatic.

Turning on his heel, Bill hesitated before lifting the curtain. He was trying to remember how many Mohmands he had seen before coming into the cave. He would have said there were five, but he had already accounted for six. There might be more ; if so, they must be dealt with swiftly, before the raiders came back from Peshawar.

Quietly he knelt down, lifted the bottom of the curtain, and peered underneath. Nothing moved beyond; the two dead Mohmands lay to left and right of the doorway.

Stepping into the outer cave, Bill picked up the rifles they had dropped, and thrust them out of sight. Then he hurried towards the mouth of the cave, gripping his two automatics. If there were any other guards, they would certainly be watching for a movement from inside the cave. Bill could expect to feel the tearing bite of a bullet the moment he was seen.

Hugging the wall, he cat-footed to the entrance. Nothing moved. No sound broke the stillness, and his spirits rose. It seemed as if his daring coup might be successful. It might be something to talk about when he was old, when he sat in the club among retired colonels, yarning of their adventures on service in Indian military stations.

He poked his head out of the cave, and immediately knew he had been too optimistic. Coming up the hillside, weary with their twenty-mile trek through the hills, were the returning raiders. Each man carried a portion of the loot, and now that they were nearing their objective their dark faces took on a new eagerness.

They were anxious to lay the booty at the feet of the Mullah, and to receive the great man's blessing.

Bill estimated their number at something over three hundred. About eighty were dressed in dusty Rajput uniforms, whilst the others wore ordinary Mohmand clothing.

The moment they realized the Mullah was in danger, one and all would be transformed into blood-thirsty fanatics, eager and willing to lay down their lives for him.

A grim smile twitched Bill's lips as he picked up the rifles and knives he had taken from the two injured Mohmand guards. He had a plan which gave him, perhaps, one chance in a hundred of getting back to Peshawar with his prisoners—for he intended to capture Orlof and the greasy-haired Yakub.

" If I fail," he thought, " I die, but the Mullah dies too."

CHAPTER THIRTEEN

IN the Mullah's cave Clay Armstrong kept his two prisoners with their backs to the wall. He did not turn his head as Bill entered.

"Everything all right?" he asked.

Bill laughed, and there was not a trace of grimness in his voice when he spoke.

"Everything is turning out just as I wanted," he said, and felt pleased when he saw stark fear show in the eyes of the Mullah. "We'll take these two gentlemen to the cave mouth . . . because they have a job to do."

"March, and no tricks," Clay ordered, and stood aside while the Mullah and the Mohmand tribesman stepped away from the cave wall.

Bill spoke grimly as he lifted the curtain to allow the two men to enter the outer cavern.

"Listen . . . you have a chance of saving many lives, your own included."

He paused, then shook his head as hope gleamed for a moment in the Mullah's eyes. "No, my lad, you aren't going to escape. Coming up the hill are your Mohmands, with Orlof and Yakub. You'll obey my orders . . . tell them just what I say . . . and if you do it nicely I'll see that you spend about fifteen years in a clean, airy prison cell . . . instead of dying suddenly on this barren Borderland."

The Mullah sneered.

"You talk big, Britisher. I can guess now who you are. You're the Secret Service man called Night, who works under cover for the Political Agent. . . . I wish I'd known earlier, I'd have made you squirm."

"Well, you didn't know earlier," Bill growled, "and not so much back-chat, or I'll make *you* squirm now. Get to the mouth of the cave and bless that mob who are coming up the hill. You'll get your orders from me . . . and if you make just one mistake . . ." He did not finish his threat aloud, but gestured with his automatics.

The Mullah stiffened, and stopped as he reached the blinding sunlight. Bill and Clay remained in the shadow. The Mullah, at Bill's orders, stood in the entrance of the cave, with the Mohmand guard by his side.

The returning raiders were now nearing the cave, and at sight of the Mullah they paused, and bowed humbly. The Mullah, conscious that three automatics were trained on him, lifted up his hands and intoned the call to prayer :

" *La illa ha illalla Muhammad Rasilalah.*"

The motley crowd of tribesmen, many of them in precarious positions on that stony hillside, bowed themselves to pray.

" Tell them to bring their loot to the edge of the ridge here," Bill hissed. " They must lay it there and retire again. Orlof and Yakub will come up and stay up."

The Mullah hesitated. He knew that most of the Mohmands would cheerfully die for him if he gave the word. Yet to give that word meant a swift bullet from behind, and the Mullah did not wish to die. He drew a deep breath, prepared to obey orders for the time being. He felt confident that the two men behind him, cool and clever though they were, could not possibly carry their impudent plan to a successful conclusion.

Before he could speak, however, the bearded Mohmand beside him took an independent line in the matter. With the agility of a gazelle this man leaped over the edge of the narrow platform in front of the cave, yelling "*Allahu Akbar !* " *

* " God is greater ! "

Rolling heavily down the stony hillside, and no doubt badly shaken, he came to a stop by a squatting tribesman and gasped out his news.

" The Mullah is a prisoner ! Two spies hold the cave ! "

The Mullah had begun to follow the tribesman, but Clay Armstrong defeated that move. He shot out of the darkness of the cave and brought the Mullah down with a tackle which would have earned him rounds of applause on any rugby ground.

From below came a moan of horror as the Mohmands saw their Mullah on the ground beneath another man. Then they charged upward, not daring to shoot for fear of hitting the Mullah. Their knives appeared as if by magic in sinewy brown hands. Let them get within striking distance of the infidels, and the insult to Mohammed's prophet would be avenged in blood.

Bill stepped out, caught the struggling Mullah by his left arm, and with a mighty heave jerked him to his feet. The Mullah quailed as he gazed into the muzzle of an automatic pistol.

" Stop 'em," barked Bill ; but the Mullah did not speak, and the nearest tribesmen were already only a score of paces away.

Clay Armstrong had thrown off his cloak, revealing his bomber's apron; he snatched out a Mills hand-grenade, pulled out the safety-pin, and whirled the missile into the air. It fell in front of the advancing men and burst with a deafening crash.

Bill bolted to the far end of the large cave, taking the Mullah with him. Clay followed as fast as he could, and the foremost Mohmands halted on the ledge before the cave mouth, dazed by the explosion and unwilling to press forward.

" One step into the cave," Bill roared, " and the Mullah dies."

As if suddenly made aware that they were in full view from inside the cave, the tribesmen vanished, leaping downhill. For a moment the two Britishers and their captive were alone.

" Think they'll attack ? " Clay asked, tossing a Mills bomb from hand to hand.

" If Orlof has anything to do with it, they will," replied Bill. " If they do, you'll die with us," he added to the Mullah. " So you'd better do some quick thinking. Your life depends on our getting safely back to Peshawar."

The Mullah's dilemma had silenced him. If he managed to persuade the tribesmen not to attack, he would be fortunate if he did not hang at Peshawar.

On the sunny hillside Orlof and Yakub were anxiously discussing the situation, while the Mohmands waited and wondered what to do. They were eager to rush the cave, yet afraid if they did some harm might come to the Mullah.

"Tell them," said Yakub the Semite, "that the Mullah cannot be harmed, and that the sooner these spies are killed the better it will be for all of us. If the Mullah *is* killed there'll be so much more for us to divide."

Orlof looked at him coldly, and spoke.

"You'd sell your own mother for a gold mohur. How do you think we'd explain the Mullah's death to these swine?"

"Then let us collect the booty, and carry it away. We can leave a guard over the cave, and starve them into submission."

Orlof made no answer. His brow was wrinkled in thought for several minutes. What happened to the Mullah he did not greatly care, but he wanted to be certain that he himself would not be injured, and that the loot from Peshawar would go with him when he left the Khyber hills.

Finally he turned to the waiting tribesmen.

"Can the beloved of Mohammed be harmed?" he asked. "Can an infidel bring to nought the will of Allah? If the Mullah's hour has come, will he quarrel with fate? Even a prophet must die once, and his great work will go on after him. He will watch over us, and stay the hand of the infidel from within the gates of Paradise."

"He speaks the truth," growled a bearded Mohmand. "Shall we stand around like children who shelter from the midday sun, while Feringhi spies sit at their ease in our very doorway? Follow me, men."

The Mohmand picked up his rifle and started uphill towards the cave. In a moment a yelling mob was straggling at his heels.

Yakub looked about him at the packages which had been brought over goat trails from the ancient city of Peshawar.

"If these were safely across the Afghan border," he muttered, "this rabble of hillmen could do what they wished."

Orlof grinned sarcastically.

"Yakub, thy blood is like water. Thy gifts are more suited to plotting than to carrying out the plots. In ten minutes the plunder should be ours to divide."

The bloodthirsty roar which betokened the decision to attack the cave brought a response from Clay Armstrong. He slipped half a dozen bombs out of the apron, took the safety-pin out of one of them, and held the lever after it had ticked three times. Three more clicks from that lever and the bomb would explode.

" I suggest, Bill," he said calmly, " that you take friend Mullah into the back cave. There may be flying fragments in here, and I wouldn't like either of you to be hit."

Bill said nothing, but rose and took the Mullah into the inner cave. He and Clay Armstrong never argued over their respective jobs. In this case Clay was handling the bombs. He could throw a Mills grenade as accurately as a crack billiards player could pot a red ball parked on the edge of a pocket.

A few seconds after Bill had vanished, the heads of several Mohmands appeared above the ledge which ran across in front of the mouth of the cave.

Clay threw his bomb, coolly and with precision. It fell and exploded a yard outside the cave. Five Mohmands in the act of rising to their feet went over backwards and rolled down the hillside, dead or wounded.

The blast of the explosion brought some shale down from the roof of the cave, and Clay coughed as the dust eddied about him.

Howls of rage arose from outside, and another group of attackers advanced. A second bomb met them and swept them off the ledge. A third and a fourth followed, and still the Mohmands came on.

" You like it, do you ? " snarled Clay, as he drew out the safety-pin of yet another bomb. " Well, try that ; you seem greedy for punishment."

This bomb fell at the mouth of the cave, on a pile of rock and shale which had been loosened from above the cave mouth. The pile vanished in a cloud of dust, and fragments smacked the wall beside Clay. He sneezed, wiped his eyes, and felt in his apron for the last bomb.

When that was gone he and Bill would be finished. No rifle fire could hold back the Mohmands.

In anxious silence Clay waited, holding down the bomb lever. The seconds dragged out to a minute and more. He could hear faint howls of rage, but for a space no more men appeared beyond the rim of the ledge.

The smoke in the cave mouth began to drift away. Clay could see far across the valley, beyond the Khyber

Pass to the snow-tipped mountains of the Safed Koh. He passed the tip of his tongue over his dry lips ; sight of the snow reminded him that he was hot and thirsty.

From the inner cave came no sound, and Clay wondered what Bill was doing. He felt sure his chief would not just be sitting twiddling his thumbs. Meanwhile, were the Mohmands hatching out some scheme whereby they could enter the cave in an overpowering throng ? Clay remembered the sight of men who had been butchered by angry tribesmen. Those long knives were terrible at close quarters.

His eyes began to ache with staring at the shape of brilliant sunlight beyond the dark cave. Suddenly one dark-skinned hand came over the ledge, gripped the stone, and was followed by another. A rifle barrel edged into view. Some one was getting ready to spring on to the ledge. Another pair of hands gripped the rock. Another rifle barrel appeared against the light brown of the distant hills.

Clay watched in silence until he could see seven pairs of hands, seven rifle barrels. He could imagine the faces below the protecting rim of rock—light-brown faces, some bearded, some almost clean shaven. Between each set of teeth would be gripped a knife.

Clay allowed the firing lever on his bomb to click up and down once more. Two seconds after he released his bomb it would explode. His nerves grew taut ; another desperate attack was coming, this time no doubt in full force.

He did not hear Bill's voice from behind until Bill spoke a second time.

" What's happening, Clay ? "

" They're going to attack, and I'm on my last bomb."

As he finished speaking seven turbaned heads rose into view. Seven Mohmands pulled themselves up on to the ledge.

Clay swung his arm back as coolly as if he were practising. As the grenade swept forward seven more heads and shoulders appeared above the ledge. The Mohmands meant to overwhelm the bomber by attacking in a series of waves. And now Clay had only one bomb with which to confront them.

CHAPTER FOURTEEN

BOOM ! The first seven attackers vanished behind a pink flash. The second wave, already half over the rocky ledge, was thrown back with them.

Clay moved forward, dragging one of his automatics out of the sash round his waist, but Bill Night grabbed him by the arm.

"Stand aside, Clay," he ordered. "It's my turn now."

"But . . . !" began Clay, and then was silent. Bill was in command, and Bill strode swiftly to the mouth of the cave, prodding the Mullah in the back to hurry him forward.

They arrived in the brilliant patch of sunlight as a third wave of attackers heaved up over the ledge. They were half over, knives held in their teeth, when they realized they were facing the Mullah. The Mullah was unharmed ! His hands were free !

Behind the Mullah was a tall broad-shouldered man in Mohmand dress. This man was smiling, and before the seven men had recovered from their astonishment he addressed them in their native Pushtu.

"Before ye advance to your deaths, look well on this man who called himself a Mullah."

Bill swung his right-hand automatic round until it almost touched the Mullah's head.

"Is this the face of a holy one who has made the pilgrimage to Mecca, and kissed the Holy Stone, and drunk the waters of the Zemzem?"

The seven Mohmands stared at the Mullah, and one of them was so amazed that he relaxed his hold and went slithering down the rocky hillside. The other six goggled at the man for whom they had been prepared to die. His face was no longer swarthy all over. Half of it was now pink and white, the colour of the skin of a Feringhi mem-sahib.

Bill could almost have chuckled. In the small cave he had washed half the Mullah's face with a preparation he had brought with him from Peshawar. This preparation had brought off every trace of the brown dye, revealing an almost schoolgirl complexion, which bore a few traces of drastic scrubbing, but allowed of no mistake.

"Do the houris wait in Paradise for those who die for a white renegade?" Bill went on. "This man has tricked you and used you as pawns in a game of his own."

" Who art thou ? " demanded one of the Mohmands. " How didst thou know this black secret ? "

Before Bill could reply a faint droning sound was heard. It grew rapidly in volume, until the air seemed to throb and quiver. Bill looked up ; from the direction of the Ali Masjid Gorge appeared six troop-carrying planes.

" Look behind thee, man of the hills," Bill said solemnly. " See the might of the Feringhi. Naught is hid from us. We are good friends, but bad enemies. Watch and tremble."

The Mohmands watched the six planes ; below them their comrades were also watching. The rocky hillside would give no cover if bombs were dropped on it.

The planes banked, heading in single file at right angles to their former course ; doors opened, and men dropped out, one after another. The Mohmands gasped as parachutes opened above the tumbling figures.

Forty-eight men alighted on the rocky terrain about three-quarters of a mile away ; the Mohmands were too astonished to fire. The parachutes were unbuckled and left on the ground ; forty-eight Bren-gunners spread out in a line and began a slow advance towards the cave. A whistle sounded, the men lifted their guns, and fired a short burst into the air.

" Tell your comrades," Bill commanded, " that mercy will be shown if ye lay down your arms. The British can be just and merciful ; they will recognize that ye have been led astray by an impostor."

The haggard Mullah flashed a look of bitter hatred at Bill. For a moment it seemed as if the Secret Service man's plea would avail. Then one or two of the Mohmands, their fighting blood roused, began to fire.

The forty-eight Bren-gunners took quick cover amid the boulders and waited for a rush. The crackle of rifle fire grew ragged, then ceased ; the Mohmands were at a disadvantage, for most of their ammunition had been expended in the sham night attack.

Nothing was left to them but surrender. Yakub and Orlof tried to persuade the men to charge, but the Mohmands, like other hill tribesmen, knew the uselessness of frontal attack against machine-guns.

A guard was left at the Mullah's cave. Bill used the Mullah's wireless set to send word to Peshawar that the Mullah was a prisoner. By nightfall the revolt in the Pass had petered out.

Bill and Clay found John Staines, and the three of them ventured through the hills under a white flag, to meet the leaders of the Shinwaris, Zakka Khels, Adam Khels, and the other tribes. There the real

Political Agent showed Orlof to the headmen as the mischief-maker who had impersonated him. A truce was arranged, and peace terms were drawn up next day, by which the tribes were deprived of the weekly fees paid to them for picketing the Pass while caravans went through. The headmen, conscious that they had been fooled by the bogus Mullah, were glad enough to accept the terms ; and once more the Khyber was opened on Tuesdays and Fridays for the passage of goods and cattle from Peshawar to Afghanistan, and from Afghan territory into India.

From papers found in the cave it was discovered that the Mullah's real name was Gabriel Stenletthen. He proved to be an adventurer employed by a European Power to make trouble on the North-west Frontier. He had used the resources set at his disposal with a double end in view, meaning under cover of the warfare he fomented to enrich himself with the wealth of Peshawar.

With the aid of Orlof, who had been a character actor in his early youth, he abducted John Staines ; and Orlof had studied the speech, appearance, and mannerisms of the Political Agent until he was able to impersonate him even in Peshawar. It was Orlof who brought about the substitution of dead pigs for silver rupees; and only the fact that Orlof's skill and courage were overmatched by those of the Secret Service men had saved the frontier from a disastrous war.

Bill Night and Clay helped to put a swift end to the trouble; and then, to their delight, they were granted six months special leave, with transit by air to England.

"We're lucky, you know," said Clay, as their train hurried them towards Karachi, where they would go aboard the British Airways flying boat. "We'll be home in time for the Cup Final. I've got a feeling that Preston North End . . ."

"Will be knocked out by now," suggested Bill Night.

Clay gave his chief a withering glance. "Listen," he said, "they were playing football in the Ribble Valley when Adam was a lad. When a London club wants a good player, where do they look for him? In the North, where all the best footballers are born and bred."

They continued to argue the respective merits of various football teams as the mighty engines of the seaplane roared into full song, and took them up from the blue-green waters of the Arabian Sea. On one point, however, Bill and Clay were agreed: they felt that they had earned the rest which lay before them.

PRINTED IN GREAT BRITAIN AT THE PRESS OF THE PUBLISHERS